CONTENTS

Copyright © Sofia Aves 2022......................III

Contents..V

Dedication VII

Chapter 1 1

Chapter 2 23

Chapter 3 45

Chapter 4 65

Chapter 5 75

Chapter 6.. 99

Chapter 7 117

Chapter 8 131

Chapter 9 147

Chapter 10 165

Chapter 11.. 181

Chpater 12 193

Chapter 13 205

Chapter 14 221

Chapter 15 231

A Note from the Author.............................. 245

Red Heart Ranch Recipies 247

Acknowledgements 257

About the Author...259

More by Sofia Aves 261

For Tony, who thankfully discovered he
wanted to be a cowboy before I turned him
into one.

CHAPTER I

Arms crossed over my chest, I stood outside the saleyards, observing the men striding around the area, their confidence obvious in their easy gate, their familiarity. A clap on the shoulder here, some smart-assed comment there, paired with a quick grin, each man so comfortable with this little patch of the world and his place in it. It was an arena I had tried to compete in again and again, and failed.

Which was why I liked my position at Red Hart Ranch, just the way it was supposed to be. Me, miles from anywhere, and anyone.

Except for the few I called family.

A kid who had to be half my weight and half my age—hell, had I ever been that young?—kicked dirt up as he walked by and winked at me from beneath a hat far too big for his lanky frame.

My teeth ground together, a dull ache bloomed across my temples as I gave him a jerky nod. I folded my arms tighter across my chest. It provided a barrier between me and the rest of the world, but the kid eyed my biceps as though I was about to cut loose on him.

I shook my head, a half-stuttered apology tumbling off my tongue that never fully materialized as he dashed away.

Damnit.

And damn Trav for sending me off home soil, even if it technically wasn't mine.

My pocket buzzed. I extracted my phone, still watching the young cowboy trail dust behind him in his escape. "Yeah."

"Jude, I think you're meant to be a bit more professional than that, you lucky bastard," Travis rebuked me from his cozy spot in front of Red Hart's fire. "You know, since you're handing out those cards and getting interest and all."

"I only just arrived. And you can shove it up your ass for not getting yours down here," I grumbled back at my best friend. "You know I hate leaving the ranch."

"It does you good. And I can't go anywhere."

That was easy to say when he was happy in his own home, right where I wanted to be. Travis and his twin sister Eve were co-owners of Red Hart Ranch, situated on the borderlands where Montana met Canada.

The edge of the wilderness, isolated and beautiful.

Travis kept asking me why I didn't have a girl in my life; I kept telling him I couldn't find one to match the land that surrounded us.

Meeting new people wasn't my forte, and my best friend knew that.

"Yeah, yeah." I rubbed my temples, but the ache persisted. "How's the leg?"

"Immobile." Trav's tone took on my side of grumpy, and I bit back a laugh. "Eve's not talking to me, and Rachel's run off."

"What'd you do to my Eve?" I said sharply. A day gone from the ranch and it was already falling apart without me there.

I should never have left.

"Your Eve? She's my sister, asshole."

"And she's the closest thing I have to one."

"That's fair." Travis sniffed. "Dammit, I hate being stuck up here."

"I hate being down here, so, you know, thanks."

"For what?"

"For sharing your pain."

"Get on with the job, Jude, then come home. You've got it covered. There's more information in your head about livestock than any man I know."

"Must be a shitty gene pool locally, then."

"I gave you something to remedy that."

4

My face burned. I resisted brushing my hand over my wallet Trav had filled with condoms in a college-level attempt to get me laid. "Yeah. How could I forget?"

Trav laughed as I hung up.

The vote of confidence was a nice reminder, but it dissipated pretty fast in the face of reality.

Get on with the job, then come home.

If only the job didn't look so damn insurmountable from where I stood.

And staying at the edge of the parking lot wasn't going to achieve a thing. I shoved my hat tighter on my head and strode through the clutter of people and livestock. My gaze trained at points away from faces. No matter how I walked, I was too ungainly, too big and awkward. So I covered myself in the grumpy persona I'd long discovered protected me best and entered the fray.

The auction yard churned with some of the wealthiest ranch owners in the north, bargaining away their livestock inside the giant, open-walled housing. Air flowed through, mingling the scent of too many men and bovine packed together in one place, though at least we were all shaded. Nevertheless, every head bore a hat, my own included. Money changed hands faster than I could keep track, their hats and boots alone worth more than half my month's wages.

Find Crossman. You'll get the best deals there.

The thin business card in my calloused hand already dogeared, Crossman's logo rough beneath the pad of my thumb. I pushed my way between haggling stock owners, wishing like hell it was Travis doing the buying, not me. Big towns, crowds, and I didn't get along. Red Hart Ranch was the only home I'd known since I was fourteen, and I didn't need a mirror to tell me that age was long past.

And here I was, playing the rancher in place of the man who should have been doing it himself—if he hadn't been incapacitated and in a cast thanks to the psychotic asshole who had changed the face of Red Hart forever.

The twins were still in recovery mode, with Trav's leg taking more time to heal than anyone expected. Thus, here I was, a deer out of the woods, my eyes wide against the oncoming headlights and frozen as fuck.

Trav had printed off a set of my own cards, stowing them safely in the branded pocket of my shirt with a grin.

Jude Mannering, Foreman.

Both of us knew mine would stay exactly where they were.

Bodies bumped me at all sides. Mumbled apologies mingled in the dying cacophony shrouded in a veil of rising dust as feet pounded the hard-packed floor. The cloying scent of bovines—unusual to a man who bred prime deer for stud—filled my head.

I jostled against an enclosure housing a rowdy cluster of cows, overwhelmed by the mass of bellowing livestock and arguing salesmen. Over my head, an auctioneer spoke through a bullhorn, or maybe it was a PA system. I couldn't tell the difference, my head already frazzled with the influx of sensory information. A knot I couldn't stretch out formed in my back.

Approaching the heart of the stockyards, I spotted Crossman printed on a large sign just beyond the rear doors of the enormous, open-ended enclosure. Why was he set up outside?

The rest of the cattle were inside...but at least I'd have fresh air if I headed out there.

I'd never listed claustrophobia as a fear, but after today, I'd consider it. By the time I made it to the far side of the saleyards, I was an expert in how not to disturb a cow.

Crossman's cattle waited in a neat cluster, quietly munching their feed just inside the rear doors. A larger banner sat outside, drawing the eye in deep browns and whites. The signwriting wasn't unlike Eve's when she rebranded Red Hart, and I wondered if the business owner had done their own work too, or hired out. Eve set the bar high, and I used that benchmark to raise my own work to her standard.

Beneath the banner, a gang of maybe a dozen handsome elk stood tall, penned alone beside a pair of branded white trucks that stood well outside the cattle area. There was no Crossman—or anyone else—in sight.

I sucked in a slow lungful of clean, fresh air, reveling in the lack of scratchy particles in my throat and the stale body odor of both men and animals that flourished inside the saleyard's enclosure.

Propping my boot lower rung, I leaned my arms over the top rail of the cattle stockade. The livestock looked healthy, but I was no expert; Red Hart had never run cattle in the fifteen years I'd lived there.

"They're good looking cattle."

I jerked against the rail, clinging to it with one clenched fist. "If you say so," I groused to hide my embarrassment at being caught daydreaming.

A head of loose brown waves surrounding a stunning face bobbed beside me. Bright eyes found mine and held. A shiver worked its way along my spine. Her skin was make-up free, though she didn't need it, and she'd used something glossy over soft, pink lips.

I closed my mouth before I said something inappropriate. Or maybe something too appropriate.

"I say so." She laughed, tossing a quick look over her shoulder. Her cheeks flushed, and I followed the pink stain as it progressed up her cheeks.

A matching grin curved my own lips. There was definitely a risk of me saying something appropriate, but flirting was too far out of my comfort zone. I lingered over the lilt in her voice—only a little different from home. It took me a moment to place it.

"You're Canadian?"

"Yep." Her lips pursed, her gaze drifted to my shirt. "You look— well, you look like you don't belong here." She raised an eyebrow in a challenge.

No apology there.

"I'm definitely not meant to be here." I clenched the railing tighter, keeping my gaze focused forward, away from the temptation planted beside me.

I studied the cow before me, but the young heifer provided a poor distraction. Dipping my chin, I broke my short-lived resolve and let my gaze wander the length of the body of the woman beside me.

Blue jeans tucked into dark tanned boots that rose halfway along slim calves. Her white work shirt was somehow pristine, despite the environment, and did nothing to hide her curves. And those eyes...they sparkled at me the whole time.

I should have stayed at home and told Travis to buy his own damn cows.

I released my death grip on the rail, turning to lean my back on it and crossed my arms over my chest instead. RHR's insignia was embroidered over the pocket. The pocket filled with pristine cards that were going to stay exactly where they were.

Curls bounced as she tipped her head back, curiosity vying with something indistinguishable in her dark blue gaze.

Flirting wasn't on the shopping list, though her curves were visible from the corner of my eye.

"How far away is that?" she asked.

I blinked.

"Too far." The place really was grating on me. "Crossman around? I thought a salesman would stay with his stock."

She turned back to the cows. One approached her outstretched hand, rubbing its nose on her fingers. The knot across my back tightened as she looked at me with those luminous eyes.

"I'm Crossman. And I never leave my stock."

Well, if I hadn't just screwed my chances of getting those cows. Maybe the girl, too.

What was that about not flirting?

If I kept lying to myself, I might even walk away from the encounter unmarred.

A muffled echo from outside drew my attention, a drone that read in my mind as out of place enough to refocus in the welcome distraction. I held out a hand to stop her talking, concentrating over the hubbub of the saleyards. Part of me recognized the cute harrumphing noise she made at the gesture, the defiant flick of auburn locks in my periphery that curled the corners of my lips.

Knowledge I store for later...assuming there was a later to be had.

The purr grew into something harsher that reverberated across the outer area where the trucks and pickups were parked but this...it sounded different, throatier, and heading in the wrong diction. Toward us. I struggled to break contact with those deep ocean blue eyes, so different from what I was used to seeing in land-locked Montana.

As the closest stall to the rear door leading to the yards, we were the first to hear the disturbance. It hadn't registered with the rest of the crowd yet, hence why no one had moved.

I swung about, taking in the blur rushing toward us and linked my arms around the woman's waist—Crossman, Ms Crossman, Mrs?—yanking us both across to the far side of her area. She shrieked, pressing tightly fisted hands to my chest, then batted at me. A shout grew in my throat, and just as I thought it might die, it broke free in a harsh yell that stilled activity around me—and within me.

The battering hands stilled at my chest. A breath, sweet and heady, brushed my cheek.

Ignoring the woman in my arms, I peered around the cows munching in their stall with little concern, unsure that I hadn't been mistaken and made a proper fool of myself.

It wouldn't be the first time, nor the last, though I had the right intention from the get go.

That same intention rarely did me well.

This time, it did.

The sharp rumble transformed to a whine that reached the ears of everyone beneath the saleyard's roofing. Yells from outside confirmed my suspicions. I jerked my head toward the south facing door we had just vacated. Midnight blue eyes broke my gaze and left my head swimming as she twisted in my hands. Soft curves moved in all the right places. Her chin bumped my shoulder to peer over it.

I stared at her, wishing I was wrong as an engine revved hard, and tires drifted across the loose dirt to shower us with grit.

Sounds from living on a large property that were all too familiar.

We cowered, and I managed to hunch over her, hoping to take the brunt of the fallout. Fine grains of sand trickled down the back of my shirt. I shook my shoulders to dislodge anything that might settle between them but only succeeded in loosening the sweat-coated dust granules as far as the waistband of my jeans.

The air froze around the open-ended shed in the quiet moment before the storm that every man in the shed recognized. Heads turned as a battered farm truck shot past us, scattering cows and people in every direction. The pickup's tail lights swerved over where we'd been standing a moment before.

A step removed from the action, we stared as the vehicle slewed across the auction yards, its occupants screaming obscenities. Beer bottles pelted onlookers and cattle alike in a melee of whoops and curses. A final puff of dust threw grit over everyone in the vicinity, and in a donut maneuver that tipped the pickup onto two wheels, it careened through the entry and disappeared.

A moment of silence held before the frozen saleyards erupted. Oddly enough, it wasn't the people who moved first.

The herd, conglomerate in their panic, stampeded.

Hooves flew in every direction, more lethal than any tire or truck. I clutched the small form huddled beneath me, my arms a solid and fragile barrier to protect a woman I didn't know but for whom I already felt some protective streak.

Or maybe that was instinct, or lust. Or both.

A holler through a megaphone or a PA system brought the knot of panic to a standstill.

Dust settled around us a second time.

Cows paused mid-stampede. Bystanders peered at the open doors, swiping grit from bared forearms. Cowboys collected hats that had scattered at the onset. Stilted chatter resumed around us as owners coaxed their livestock back to their places and resurrected downed enclosures.

Movement against my chest returned my attention to the woman in my arms. She twisted around to stare up at me with cobalt eyes the perfect shade of a clear winter day. Some semblance of grace left me with a day that had started so poorly but ended so well.

She arched back, her chin tipped up toward me. Her lips parted, the tip of her tongue visible between them.

It took me a moment to realize she was speaking. I dipped my head under the pretense of too much background noise. Those pouty lips pressed into a line, then she smiled.

"I said, you can let me up now, cowboy."

"Jude," I murmured, watching her lips move, my own tingling in response. I curved my hands around her waist, squeezing just a little. "My name is Jude."

"Oh." She wiggled against me.

I played with the brief thought of pulling her closer, but one sharp, darkened look told me it would be a mistake. I loosened my arms around her.

Ms—I hoped to hell it was Ms or Miss— Crossman stepped back, running a hand over her hair. Dust motes hung in the air, but that wasn't what made it difficult for me to breathe. Her curves seemed to be emphasized by the action in the background while for me she moved in slow motion. Grit and straw stuck out haphazardly, her white shirt coated in a fine layer of dust.

"Natalie."

"Natalie." I squeezed her slightly roughened hand in mine, taking in her clean but crumpled form as she straightened, sweeping her hair back from her face with no fuss. The line of her jaw held true as she surveyed me.

The chaos surrounding us crept into my consciousness. "Give me a sec?"

She paused in her own clean up and nodded.

Her assessing gaze weighed on me as I helped erect nearby enclosures and herd wayward cattle back to their places. Men chatted as we worked, and I was a good quarter of an hour into the solution before I realized my self-conscious attitude had deserted me. I worked shoulder to shoulder with the men around me, men who either worked land on a regular basis or directed the men around them. As for the different breeds, I realized they didn't hold quite the same appeal as home. Cattle weren't for me.

Travis had sent the wrong man.

What should—could—have been a panic attack miles from home didn't happen. Instead, I focused on what needed to be done and put my back into it. I relished the muscle strain of lifting and carrying temporary fencing, the understanding that grew in me of what it meant to move more stubborn animals than I was used to herding. That knot in my stomach, the tenseness in my shoulders lessened somewhat.

Instead, I accepted the situation and moved on.

On occasion I glanced across the space. Dark hair flicked around her as she encouraged her stock and others to return to their places and helped rebuild the enclosures. She worked her stock on her own while a young man loitered outside near her banner there. When she was finished with her first group of stock, they worked the elk into their own enclosure.

I shook my head, wondering how I was going to choose the right stock for Red Hart when all I could see were curves and sienna dark curls.

Finally, the temptation overwhelmed my need to help. I wound my way through the dismantled saleyards, giving a quick hand to erect downed enclosures and bypassing others. Finally, I returned to her stall and studied her.

"Maybe we should see to your animals?" The knot in my stomach tightened, but not for the same reasons as before. I gestured to a few of her cows who had gotten loose from her makeshift enclosure.

Under my gaze, she backed away one small step at a time.

"Um. Yes. That sounds good." A blush rose in her cheeks, giving her a glow amongst the dirt and muck. She spun on her heel, bumping into the railing she's tentatively set up.

I smiled to myself, watching her soothe the ansty cattle as they stomped in circles. After a moment, I yielded, shouldering a bale of hay and tossing it over the fence. I tugged at the string and the cows dived in.

"Not much different from any other animal, are they?"

The cows attacked their feed, but nothing about them drew me. Their large eyes held none of the intelligence of our own famous red deer. But different times meant either diversifying, or potentially allowing the ranch to fail.

That wasn't happening on my watch.

"Not a real cowboy, are you?" She grinned, joining me at the rail. A caramel coloured beast snuffled her shirt.

I glanced at her from the corner of my eye.
"I'm supposed to be looking for good stock to
take home. But—" I gestured to the chaos
behind us. "I'm well out of my depth."

"You want a quick masterclass on
bovines?" The sparkle was back in her eyes.

An answering grin spread over my face,
though my stomach took a plummet, leaving
me in freefall. "You bet."

CHAPTER 2

Half an hour later I had more facts than I needed stuffed into an already straining skull. My moment of comfort reduced significantly as the saleyards resumed their usual activity. I nodded for the dozenth time, and a wry smile curved Natalie's soft pink lips. Well, pink. I couldn't speak for the soft part yet.

I blinked at the stray thought that slid through my mind and stayed put.

"I've lost you, haven't I?" Natalie tilted her head back, catching me in that opal dark gaze again. A small smile, sweet, sexy and not at all unkind only highlighted her cheekbones, but it was those tender-looking pink lips that floored me.

I needed to touch them, and find out if they were as soft as I thought they would be.

Her smile turned coy, and my mind stopped working altogether.

Get it together, Jude. You haven't been a lovelorn teen for over a decade.

Actually, I'd never been a lovelorn teen. Not since I decided to run from a dysfunctional home at fourteen and set out to get as far from the southern states as I could possibly get without requiring a passport.

"Probably." I scuffed up dirt that landed on someone else's boot.

A pristine and unmarked boot of the shelf variety.

I looked up into a clean shaven face with no lines and an even suntan. The cowboy, who was at least ten years younger than me, gave me a saucy wink better suited to a club girl than a saleyards, but what did I know? Hell, I was getting old.

24

"Listen to Nat. She knows her stuff." An unwrinkled blue shirt was strung across wide shoulders and accompanied by a clean white hat that perched on his head like it had been made for him.

It probably was.

The younger cowboy leaned over the railing, muscles popping beneath his shirt like he was on a photo shoot.

I abstained from looking around and miraculously managed not to retreat into myself.

"So I hear. She's good?"

He winked at me. "The best sort."

Get off the rail before I take it out of your hands.

The somewhat violent thought ripped a burning trail through my head before I could stop it.

"Of course it is." I pivoted to face Natalie, presenting my back to the younger man and jammed my hat on my head. "Thank you for everything. I'll...go digest it all for a bit. See

25

what suits the ranch." My lips formed a tight smile I didn't bother to fight.

Natalie's dark blue glance flitted over my shoulder. "I might have to work for a bit but...coffee later? Do you drink coffee or would lunch be better— no, make that dinner?"

I smiled, and hoped she wasn't doing it out of pity. "Dinner sounds great. I'll be around—" I gestured to a peaked roof visible from beneath the saleyard's tented covering. "Probably at the bar over there or downstairs somewhere."

Her eyes lit with a sparkle that hit me well above the belt, rather than below. The shock sucked all the air from my lungs in an instant.

"Drinker?"

"I'd say yes but not really. Eve managed to get me into whiskey tastings for a bit." I grinned, still trying to work out how much she'd be out of pocket for the whiskey collection Red Hart now sported, though I wasn't convinced it was all for me.

Eve liked a nightcap as much as anyone at Red Hart, seasonal hand or not. Now, at least, we could accommodate most tastes.

"Eve, huh?" That navy gaze narrowed, flashing at me as she looked over my shoulder, her wide smile greeting her next customer who dipped his head to brush his lips across her cheek, his hand in a familiar clasp at her waist.

When the not-so-stranger raised his head there was more than a challenge in his dark gaze—something akin to possession.

I didn't bother to look back at the young man. Dust rose from where I kicked the dirt a little harder than I needed as I left the saleyards, without what Travis had sent me to find, and my head full of knowledge I hoped I never needed.

Wooden doors swung gently as I passed through them into a timewarp, certain there would be at least one more murder at Red Hart when I got back to question Travis on his logistical capabilities.

Maybe I should have taken Eve up on her offer to sort accommodation, but I'd likely have ended up at some resort a large town away doning fluffy slippers. The back of a truck suited my meager needs just fine. I doubted they would have liked a dusty, gritty cowboy in the midst of their lounge, and I certainly wasn't going to sip champagne.

I had more to thank Travis for than I thought.

Presenting my back to the crowd, I stared over the bar. An almost too-hot fire flickered beside me, caging me in but giving me relief from the hubbub that filled the space with too many bodies for my liking.

Frankie Laine's 'Dead Man's Hand' serenaded the crowd huddled around the bar. The place had a distinct rumble that covered me as I pushed my way to the bar and ordered from a Cat Ballou look-alike.

Even the staff dressed in theme.

I'd half expected a busty showgirl serenading us from her perch on a piano. In my instant fantasy, the showgirl's hair draped over her in auburn waves around her, and when she turned doe-eyes on me I was staring at

Natalie's face. I shook my head, but half a beer later, I still couldn't dispel the image, wondering if I'd remembered her curves right.

The memory of another man's hands on her ripped through my mind, and I forced my brain to tinker on something other than silk curls and sexy as sin curves.

I'd expected the rest of the cowboys would head home with their earnings or their new stock after the saleyards closed, but their presence in the town—or at least, in the saloon bar—had doubled. My shoulders hunched forward, and I leaned over my beer as the chatter grew more raucous.

A body bumped me from behind. I knew before I turned it was a female. I twisted, so ready to see her again, but all I saw was a swathe of blonde hair that disappeared between patrons as she wove her way back to wherever she had come from.

"Sorry," I muttered to my beer as I turned back to the bar. My phone vibrated in my jeans, and my spine stiffened with every buzz. I drew it out of my pocket with tight hands, finally drawing my gaze from the fire that flickered merrily before me.

A message flashed up on the screen, and I swore I could smell the holly and snow that came with Red Heart, maybe topped with a side of the ham and baked vegetables Eve had likely put out as a large spread for the hand and permanent residents of the ranch. Hell, I missed being home.

Not being at Red Hart was akin to me as leaving the state, maybe the country.

Eve: Did you survive the madhouse?

Me: Think I'm still in it.

Eve: Take your time. Get everything sorted. Don't worry about anything.

Me: ... ...

Staring at the screen yielded zero results. And telling me not to do something always had the opposite effect; Eve knew that. My mind went into overdrive, fussing on the same useless damn thought like an old woman in a knitting circle talking about the neighbors—and that brought another worry to the forefront of my brain.

Black Hill had been gnawing at the fence lines like a mangy dog with the last bone on earth since before last Christmas. If there was something that could go wrong, now was the worst time with me away and Trav laid up. Not that Eve wasn't at all capable, but as much as she tried to be a one woman army, there were just some things that family could do better when we were all together.

Damn, I hate being away from the ranch.

I pressed my lips together tight and pocketed my phone without sending anything back. Whatever platitudes Eve needed to hear, they could wait until tomorrow.

"Not your usual?" Gage, a cowboy who had come up from the south in search of work, asked as he hunched over the bar a few spots along. A long, thin scar raked his face from eyebrow to just below his jaw. What might have become twisted on another man gave him an air of competence, of a man who had taken the bull by both horns and lived to walk away.

He'd spoken to me when his drink was placed in front of him, though so far I had only seen his side profile. The deep scar rent his tanned skin from cheekbone to jaw line where it divided his few day's growth in a stripe of white. He studied the contents of his glass.

I pushed down the urge to ask him what had happened. If he was anything like me, he wouldn't appreciate a stranger prying into his life. "No more than yours, I imagine. What are you doing so far north?"

"Lookin' for work. One ranch closed up. Been there for a bit. Used to be military." He grimaced. "Got some seasonal jobs, and someone pointed me up here."

My ears pricked. "How are you with animals?"

"I've learned to fucking hate bulls." He grimaced and mimed tumbling off an imaginary bull's back. "Cows are all right, I haven't found anything else that hates me as much as a bull with an eight second grudge."

I laughed, thinking of young Will Kirk who had worked a season or two at Red Hart and headed off chasing his own rodeo fame and fortune. A sense of solidarity sank between us. "I know a guy you'd get on with well. Manage to stay on 'til the bell?"

"Once."

"Still, not bad. No chance in hell I'd get on one."

"Smart man." He eyed me speculatively. "Where you from?"

"North." I placed my glass on the bar and opened my mouth to offer the man a job when a bundle of silky dark waves that glittered garnet red beneath the saloon bar lights draped over my forearm.

"Whiskey ditch, please." Ocean blue eyes turned my way, fixed on me with a sparkle that was all her own. "Glad you made it out alive."

My stomach took a dive as I was swept away into the depths of her bottomless gaze.

Gage wiggled his eyes at me and turned to the man on his other side.

I snorted. So much for solidarity. "Expected me to turn tail and head back up the mountains, did you?" My fingers raised of their own volition, gliding beneath one of her long curls where it rested on my forearm. It slid softly over roughed skin as I wrapped it around my finger and gave it a playful tug.

My plummeting stomach hit ground level, birthing an ache that shot straight to my groin.

"It might surprise you but no." Natalie unwrapped her hair from my finger. The back of her hand brushed mine in a slow caress.

I couldn't tell if it was intentional or not.

Her drink thumped down in front of her, and I signaled the bartender to bring a second one my way.

"And here I thought you had written me off." My self confidence took a similar path as my stomach had earlier. I downed the rest of my beer and pushed the empty glass away from me. Froth slid down the inside to pool at the base.

"Why would I do that?" Natalie's brow furrowed.

"Dunno."

And now I was reduced to the conversational aptitude of a boulder.

Fucking brilliant.

"Mmm."

I sensed Natalie's attention still on me and risked a sideways glance. Blue eyes stared back, unyielding with a side serve of speculation.

My lips formed a tight line. "What?"

"You know what I think you need?"

"To get some cows and go home?"

"Relax, Jude. That's all. And I think I know just the thing."

I raised an eyebrow. "Of course you do."

"You're staying here, not heading home?" She ran the tips of her fingers around the rim of her glass. A quiet song emanated from every circuit her fingers made, barely audible over the hum of the crowd and the truly atrocious bluegrass that blared across the bar.

"Yeah." I coughed, clearing my abruptly parched throat. "I thought I'd stick around and try to build some bridges. Professional relationships. Not that I'm particularly good at those." I grimaced into my whiskey.

"You're doing pretty well so far."

"I'll take your word for it."

"You will, Mister Foreman. You're doing a better job than you think."

"I am?" I raised an eyebrow and twisted to face her, bracing my forearm on the bar. The movement blocked out the rest of the room, so all I could see was Natalie and the flames flickering behind her.

It was a damn fine view.

Red glinted from her mesmerizing waves. I curled my hands into fists to repress the temptation to touch her again. Her lips parted in a half-smile as she tilted her head a little to look up at me, exposing the slender column of her throat, the gentle curve covered by her pristine white shirt.

How she managed to stay so clean amongst such filthy cattlemen, I had no idea.

She tipped her head back, her eyes sparkling with a renewed challenge. Body odor and stale beer wafted around me, but Natalie brought a breath of icy, fresh mountain air with her wherever I saw her. It reminded me of home.

I swallowed hard.

"Yes. Dance?" Natalie held out a slim hand.

I struggled to brush back the dual hit of heart ache and arousal for a long minute before the whiskey kicked in and I shot mine back the way she had had hers.

I mean, what's the worst that can happen?

Her palm was just rough enough to graze mine, a reminder she was a hard-working girl from the right side of the tracks for me. I followed the jerk of her head toward the empty space behind us. Darkness filled the windows that faced the street front. Lights had dimmed, and facing the fire, I hadn't noted the sunset or the time that had passed.

Dance? Me?

The only thing I was good at dancing around was an antsy deer. My stomach plummeted further. I expected to see the thing fall out on the floor anytime now.

My lips twitched, ready with a negative response. A fist grazed my shoulder hard enough to leave a bruise.

"Jude's a regular Astaire. He'd love to."

I shot Gage a hard look over my shoulder and mentally rescinded the job offer.

The scarred cowboy sent me a shit-eating grin right back and raised his glass.

"Perfect," Natalie purred. She caught my hand and entwined her fingers in mine.

I looked down at our joined hands, bemused. She shot her whiskey back, and I followed her lead, something about trends in Rome niggling at the back of my mind.

She dragged me onto the dance floor, the sharp, warm tang of whiskey still on the back of my tongue and linked her arms around my neck.

My body zinged from boots to stubble as she pressed her petite frame to mine, and I got to relish those curves up close and personal. I sucked in a breath and got a lungful of fresh air.

"I swear you bring the mountains with you. Where are you from?" The too-honest words tumbled from my lips. I hadn't managed to ask before I'd walked away earlier in the day. My manners had been woeful. Maybe getting off the ranch had been a good thing after all and gave me a chance to kick my ass into gear.

"North."

"Funny, that's what I say." I paused, settling my hands lightly on her waist where her hourglass figure dipped in violent curves. "We're border country. Top middle. 'Bout as middle as you can get, actually."

She swayed against me, with me as we moved in tiny steps, learning each other's rhythm. Well, I learned her rhythm, as I didn't have one of my own to speak of. Her head tilted back, and she watched me with a furrowed brow.

I wanted to lean down and kiss the lines away.

"Well, then. You must be..." Her nose wrinkled, and she raised an eyebrow. "Black Hill?" Her tone held a doubtful note.

I wasn't surprised; Black Hill had a reputation for being both ruthless and careless—not the sort you wanted as a neighbor, and unfortunately, they were ours.

"Hell, no. Sorry. Red Hart. We take better care of the land than damn Bill MacQuaid. Ah. Language. Sorry."

"MacQaid is an asshole of the first order." Natalie laughed at the shock that must have been written across my face. She swayed her hips so her front brushed across my groin.

I repressed a groan as I hardened. Hell, I'd need a cold shower just to get off the dance floor. Maybe I could get Gage to douse me in a picture of cold beer, though it would be a waste. It seemed to be the sort of thing that would be right up his alley.

A rueful grin worked its way across my face. I hadn't expected to actually socialize on the impromptu trip. Yet after only meeting the hands who came to help out at the ranch and the very rare trip into our local small town of White Cap two hours south, here I was making new friends like they were going out of fashion. Totally out of my comfort zone, and apparently thriving.

Maybe Trav knew what he was doing after all.

"So you know Black Hill, but I haven't heard of you before. How is that?"

"You're not one of the twins, are you?" Natalie asked. Her gaze narrowed the tiniest bit.

"Nope. Foreman. Farm fixture."

Auburn waves brushed her rosy cheeks as she nodded. "That makes sense," she murmured so low I could barely hear her over the music.

"Does it?"

"Yup." She wiggled her shoulders and pressed a little closer. "I wondered, when you spoke about Eve before."

I had? I wracked my brain, but I couldn't recall anything I'd said or much about the afternoon, apart from meeting Natalie and a bunch of rampaging cows. And then my head had been filled with thoughts of her alone, and I hadn't focused on anything else after that.

The song ended and another started. The pounding beat was more suited to a city than a saloon bar, but the lighting darkened further and people flocked to crowd the space.

Why they needed to be in mine I couldn't work out.

A body jostled me, and a stray elbow attacked my kidneys.

I lurched slightly before my balance kicked in. My arm around her waist tightened, and I pulled her closer into me where she fit perfectly thigh-to-thigh.

A soft gasp, or maybe it was a sigh, slipped from her lips to brush mine in the ghost of a kiss.
Her eyes flared wide as I dipped my head deeper to graze my lips over the shell of her ear. "Are you okay?"

"Mmhmm." Her response reverberated through her chest to mine. "You want out of the crowd?"

"How could you tell?" My lips curved in a smile against her cheek she couldn't see.

"Because you're holding onto me like a lifeline. No, don't you dare," she warned when I loosened my grip on her waist. "Got a place to stay?"

I winced. "Flatbed of my truck under a starry sky?" I tacked the last part on to make it sound more romantic than effectively admitting I was a vagrant.

It wasn't that I was too tight in the hip pocket to shell out for a room, more that the thought of staying in rooms that were essentially matchboxes stacked on top of each other closed my chest to the point of zero lung capacity.

"Mmm, I thought you might be roughing it. Come on. I have a trailer with heating that's got room for both of us. Not much but...you won't wake up with an itchy back."

I didn't admit her that I'd crossed the country in my first truck doing just that, and had never managed to break the habit.

Natalie unwound herself from my arms in a fast turn that left me dizzy and towed me off the dance floor.

Gage raised an eyebrow, his scar stretching as he smirked at me.

"Stay in town," I yelled over the music as I was dragged out the door.

"What the hell for?" he yelled back.

"I got a job for you!"

Surprise widened his eyes, twisting the thin scar that ran from brow to jawline as Natalie succeeded in evicting me from the building.

Cold night air slapped my cheeks as I tried to work out the best way to tell her I was too damn old for a one night stand.

My last had been a long time ago, and I hadn't cared about that crazy ass woman half as much as I already did the one towing me around in pure cave woman style.

She threw a cheeky glance over her shoulder as though reading my mind, and my resolve broke a little.

Maybe it was time to form some new habits after all.

CHAPTER 3

Montana night air slammed into me, and for once, it wasn't from Natalie. It did, however, give me a reality check I didn't want or need. I squeezed her hand tight, tugging her to a halt across the deserted main road. I was glad for the lack of audience as Natalie turned to face me. The sparkle dimmed from the deep abyss of her gaze, the lines returning to her forehead.

I brushed my thumb across them until they cleared, and leaned forward to brush my lips over the same spot on her brow. "Natalie. I'm not sure this is a good idea. I don't—"

I don't do one night stands was never going to come out right no matter how I phrased it. My inclination to just take her to my truck and fuck her senseless had greatly reduced without an excess of spirits and warmth.

"You don't what, Jude? Have a little fun in the middle of nowhere? How many girls do you get at that ranch, and how many of them have you fucked recently?" Natalie arched an eyebrow.

She left me speechless for a moment. One single, thoughtless moment, and I was screwed.

"None. No. That's an outright lie."

"Thank you."

"No, really. I don't remember the last time screwing someone was just a—" Another outright lie. One I could pretend to cover, though I suspected Natalite saw right through my facade.

"You don't know the last time you cared? Is that it? The last time you had a broken heart? Guilting away that you fuck and forget, Jude? I promise you that you won't fuck and forget me."

She was right up in my face. Her chest heaved with the vehemence of her words, her body swaying toward me, and God help me, there was no way I was going to be able to say no to her.

"No. I'll never forget you, whether I take you to bed or not."

She snorted. "Take me to bed? You have a truck, Jude."

"I have stars?" I offered, and held out my hand.

It was the worst fucking decision I had ever made, but I extended that somewhat wilted olive branch, and I didn't retract it.

"Okay," she whispered. "I can do stars, but it's really damn cold. I have heating and a mattress? Without straw?"

"If it's what you need." I realized the moment the words were out of my mouth how caustic they were. "We could do stars later? Or next time? Red Hart gives you the most amazing— ahhh." I ground the sound out as her fingers brushed the length of my cock through my jeans, already hard as hell and straining in its confines.

"So there will be a next time."

"Do you want there to be a next time?"

"I think I do. And I think I have my answer right here." She sent me a mischievous smile laden with desire of her own.

"Hell yes," I groaned.

She cupped my balls through my jeans, scrapping her short nails over them as though the denim wasn't in the way of her caress.

Every sensation hit me as though I were bare.

I pulled her roughly against me. "Stop, Natalie. You don't know me."

"I know you, Jude. Do you know yourself?"

You've known me for a few damn hours and already you're under my skin.

A solitary stare into her dark eyes and I slammed my mouth against hers.

Her soft whimper drove me higher. I pulled her into me as I traced the line of her lips with my tongue. A groan of my own reverberated inside my chest as she opened her mouth and let me in.

I found the perfect curves of her ass with my palms, pulling her up against me. "Tell me where, sweetheart."

Her breath hitched and for a too-long moment I wondered if she was going to push me away, tell me to cool off in the damn Mississippi.

Natalie paused and shook her hair back. "I don't start something I intend to stop. If that's what's happened to you, then I'm very sorry. But do you have any misgivings about them?" The defiant tilt of her chin softened a fraction. "Unless you don't want to, of course?" Her ocean eyes deepened in color as she searched mine.

I untangled my fingers to cup her cheeks. "No. There is no uncertainty here." To my great surprise, those words weren't a lie. Nothing in the gentle curve of her face showed me that what she said was false either, and I dipped my head to kiss her sweetly.

That lasted less than five seconds.

The moment our lips met, fireworks went off in my brain. I was half conscious of Natalie dragging me across the deserted saleyards. Every light was off in the few surrounding vans. I hadn't realized how late it had gotten, or how long I'd danced with her.

Her mouth grazed mine and she urged me forward. I cinched her waist too tight as her large, white trailer came into view at the edge of the light thrown by the town.

Natalie scrubbed every errant thought clean from my brain as she turned back to me, her head tilted back, her lips parted.

It was too much of an invitation and far too damn hard to resist.

I spun her on the spot, catching those slim wrists. She moved with me, onto her toes as she rose against my chest. Her eyes flared wide beneath luxurious lashes, her chest rising and falling in an irregular rhythm.

I backed her to the side of the trailer and pinned her with one knee pressed between her thighs. Lifting her wrists over her head with both hands, my fingers pressed to her palms to prevent her reaching for me.

She mewled, arching up. Her need ruined me, etched into me. I laughed softly, desperate to taste those soft damn lips.

Mountain freshness mingled with Montana night air, whirling around in my head, or maybe with the whiskey. My mouth pressed to hers in an anything but gentle kiss, and she responded with hungry lips.

The warmth of her body seeped through my open jacket, pushing the cold away as she pressed close to me. I sent a silent prayer heavenward that I'd gotten her trailer right and that some very angry cowboy wasn't going to emerge while I got my rocks off.

"This is yours, right?" I wound my hands into her hair, and tugged gently at the roots. The pads of my thumbs turned small, firm circles at the base of her neck.

"Uh huh," Natalie moaned into my mouth.

"Good." I pressed her firmly against the side of her truck and slid my knee between hers, pushing her feet apart.

So much for no one night stands.

That single thought sent my resolve flying out the proverbial window. I might regret it later, but right now all I needed was her.

I tugged at the waistband of her jeans with one hand until the soft cotton of her shirt exposed warm, bare skin that turned to gooseflesh instantly. I didn't object to it, tracing my fingers over her side.

Unfortunately she did.

Natalie let out a cute little yelp that only fuelled my desire.

"Inside, please. It's fucking freezing out here." She begged in the sweetest little way, her head tilting back when I tugged at her hair. A soft mewl slipped from her mouth.

I tapped her feet apart to press my hips to her, grinding her back into the side of the trailer. "If that's what you need, sweetheart," I murmured.

She fumbled to extract a single key from her pocket and fought with the lock.

I slipped my arms around her waist and swept her hair over her shoulder. The action exposed her shoulders to me. I slid one hand between the curve of her breasts to unbutton the offending material and pushed it aside. Her still-warm skin tasted of salt and something sweet, like honey or vanilla. I trailed my mouth over the slope where her neck joined her shoulder and memorized every sensitive spot there that earned me a moan or a sigh, tucking the information away for later.

I tested it out a few more times before the door flung open. Natalie stumbled in my arms, and I took a step back with her to prevent both of us falling back on our combined ases.

"Nice work."

Natalie huffed. "If you say so."

"I do say so."

She kicked off her boots and leapt up to toss them inside the cab before she swung around and slipped into a pod sleeper behind it. I followed her lead, placing my boots in the passenger side footwell and slipped into the small room after her. I pulled the door closed behind me and was engulfed in pure darkness.

"Natalie." I waited for an answer, but when none came, I cleared my throat.

Her lilting giggle turned my attention to my right, and when I reached for her, I encountered bare flesh not more than two feet away. I wrapped my arms tight around her waist and drew her into me. "Damn, sweetheart. Eager?"

"Mmhmm." Her silken waves brushed over my forearm as I shucked my jacket to the floor and undid my cuffs.

My shirt and jeans followed in short order to create an imaginary heap. I tucked the foil packet I'd extracted between my fingers so as not to graze her skin, my cheeks blazing at the memory of Trav shoving a lifetime's supply into my wallet. But he didn't belong in this room with us, and I shoved his echoing laughter away and buried it deep. Natalie was who mattered, not some prank my best friend had played in a not-so-subtle hint.

Darkness enveloped us, lifting every sensation, though the lack of familiarity with the tiny room that seemed so much bigger threw me. I nudged for the bed with my knees as I braced an arm around her back.

"Damn, sweetheart. I could use a light?"

"I—Can we go without it? Maybe I'm not scared of the dark with you here."

I frowned, brushing my lips over her frown. The furrowed lines bumped against my lips, but I let it go. If she wanted the lights out, I wasn't going to be the asshole who said no.

"Next time, I want to see you," I murmured the words into her ear, and flicked my tongue against her lobe.

Her low moan turned me to pliable clay. Her knees buckled, and she would have dropped, had I not kept a tight hold of her.

"Okay," she whispered, breathless, though the single word wobbled a little. "Next time."

I smiled against her skin and tucked the information away to look at later. Right now I needed her in a very different way, one I thought she wouldn't mind.

The bed hit my thigh. I pulled her tight into my chest as I fell forward, taking her off her feet. I kept her braced until my outstretched hand hit the soft blankets folded on top and then I let us both crash down together.

My straining cock brushed against her slick, swollen flesh as I pressed myself between her thighs, resting there. A primal growl rose in my throat, threatening my control. I squeezed the blankets into a tight fist, and breathed out a slow, long breath. She wiggled beneath me, a tiny movement that frayed my control. I shoved it down, sliding my free hand between the swell of her breasts to cup the back of her neck, angling her head just the way I wanted her.

"Fuck, Nat. You're drenched."

Her body moved, undulating beneath me as she mumbled something that started as a stutter. Her skin warmed beneath the base of my palm. I imagined her flush as I found her mouth and swallowed her next words.

Her skin had cooled without contact. I covered her with my body, willing my heat into her bones. The lack of light heightened my other senses. Her sweet and fresh scent engulfed the space, paired with the honey sweetness of her arousal. I memorized every curve of her where she pressed to me, the taste of her skin. Whiskey and honey, and all things safe and home.

My breath caught at the thought though it was dashed away when her nails stroked along the length of my cock. I tore the foil pack open and rolled the rubber over me.

"Can I?" she asked softly, still circling my length with sweet little grazes that left me aching, my balls already drawn up tight.

"If that's what you want," I grated out through clenched teeth. Relinquishing control, I braced one forearm either side of her head.

Light fingers stroked over me, teasing and discovering as she went on her own little tour. I recited the National Anthem backward in my head, though I only made it to the second verse.

I caught her hand, stilling her movement before I did lose control.

"That's enough, Natalie." My voice came out harsh even to my ears. I dipped my head to kiss her slow and deep, until she made another one of those little sigh-moans that had become my new addiction. "I want to last for you. Not rush this."

You deserve so much more than a quick fuck and a snoring body.

And no matter the cost, I was determined to make sure that didn't happen tonight. She rolled the rubber over me, her fist closed at my length as she jacked me twice.

I failed to hold back my own moan, squeezing her waist tight.

She laughed softly as she hooked her legs around my hips and shoved at my shoulders to flip me onto my back. I sucked in air as mine whoosed from my lungs. The combination left me light headed as she jacked me again, rubbing my covered cock head over her hot little pussy.

"Girl, you're a little minx," I groaned.

Natalie shifted on top of me, her limbs a tangle in the darkened room, and all I could imagine with an octopus of a woman turning circles on my stomach. Her thighs pinned either side of my hips and she straddled me.

I dropped my hands to catch her knees and found her feet. "What's this—"

Natalie laughed again and slapped my calf. My addled brain finally figured out which way she was facing. Reaching forward, my hands made it to her hips before she lowered herself onto me.

I gripped her tight, halting her progress. "Are you planning to torture me?"

"Only a little." Her hair ficked teasingly over my wrist.

"Because having a girl ride me reverse and not be able to see my cock slide between those gorgrous fucking ass cheeks might ruin me."

"And here I thought I was being economical."

"You what?"

"Something about 'save a horse, ride a cowboy'?" She jacked me one last time and slid over me a bare inch, her words lost in her moans.

Holy mother of God. Let me save the wild horses.

I gripped her hips tight, controlling her drop. When she lifted again I held her down, making her impale herself on me in an inexorable, controlled descent. I didn't go too fast, or too slow, letting her get used to the feel of me inside her. I cursed softly in a wordless string as I pushed her down, both my torture and hers.

She whimpered, her thighs trembling where they wrapped around mine until I pushed her all the way to my hilt and held her there. Soft skin brushed my balls, her arousal coating us both. Her hips bucked a little in my hold, but I kept her still, pinning her to me until she tilted forward a little. She clasped her hands around my thighs, pushing up, and I let her.

Nat undulated as she rose, tight along my length, then plunged down. A small scream tore from her lips as she rose and dropped again, making the same, tormented cry each time. I gripped her thigh, needing to hold her but let her move, to seek her own pleasure while I tried not to focus on mine.

And in the darkness kind of prayer I'd been waiting to hear.

"Fuck me please, Jude."

It was less whisper but more than a sigh.

I gently pushed her down a little harder, her arousal making my part easier. Her fingers wrapped around mine as her hair tangled our interlaced hands. Pleasure built around us both, her moans mingling with mine as I pushed up. Her thighs trembled, squeezing tighter. Tremors rocked her body and it quaked as she clenched down hard around me.

I held onto her tight while her pussy pulsed, the waves of pleasure that rolled through her matching her cries until they drifted away. Her clenches reduced to light flutters, the aftershocks of her orgasm leaving her sated and liquid, draped over my thighs.

I gathered her in my arms to pull her back against my chest. "Damn, sweetheart. That was something incredible." I swept damp curls from her face and tilted her chin back to claim her mouth, still inside her and as needy as she had been a moment before.

I wound my arms and legs around her, letting her catch her breath then rolled us both so her head was where mine had been a moment before, but she faced the pillow, and my hips pressed to the glorious fucking curve of her ass.

Still inside her, I surged forward, relishing her shriek, the way her body picked up where it had left off right after her last orgasm. She arched into me, but I pushed her hair over her shoulder to expose her back to me.

I moved slowly inside her, long and too slow, even for me, though I needed to last for her. Dipping my head, I drew my nose over the curve of sensitive skin I'd discovered where her shoulder and neck joined, tracing back and forth with my lips.

Natalie moved with me, whining as she tried to press back for more until I filled her, pinned to the mattress. Arching back, I stroked my tongue along her spine to the nape of her neck, and she screamed softly.

Moving to my own rhythm, I did it again and again, surging forward, licking to the music of her over sensitized screams until she was a trembling mess beneath me.

"Jude, please—" she choked on a gasp, shuddering against me, sexy and beautiful. Her body arched, taut with pleasure, and she threw her head back into the curve of my shoulder. The trembling that had preceded her first orgasm rippled through her body.

I speared my hand into the mattress and slid my other hand along her body and between her legs, only just managing to maintain my rhythm. Her body was slick with sweat and arousal. I spread it around her clit, tracing around and around the tiny bundle of nerves. Her keening, constant cry told me she was close. I waited until the little nub hardened, then brushed my thumb over it. Back and forth, back and—

She came apart in my arms. Straining, her head curved back as she pressed into my hand, then rocking back with the need to feel me inside her. Her desperation became a frenzy, her entire body shaking. Her forehead dropped back to the mattress, and she heaved great, deep breaths.

I didn't stop, riding the height of the wave with her before I descended into my own oblivion.

CHAPTER 4

I cracked an eyelid open. Light filtered through the seam of the door in a thin line, just enough to see the outline of the stunning woman draped across my chest. The distinct addition of sunlight gave me a sense of unreality. Natalie's presence anchored me. And though it was our first—and potentially only—morning together, she was in exactly the right place. I savored the languid weight of her, spread across my body like she'd always been there.

Her legs tangled in mine. She'd wrapped one arm tight around my chest, as best she could. Her other hand rested just below my shoulder.

If there was any day to sleep in, today was it. But gauging from the pale light seeping through the door to her king single sleeper, the sun was just rising, and that meant plenty of activity. I didn't want her to emerge disheveled in front of a group of cowboys, each who likely had less manners than the last, or have her branded loose when I walked out behind her, having met her the day before.

I untangled my fingers from her hair, attempted to avoid catching my roughened knuckles in knots, but the silken strands tumbled between my hands to curl on her bare back. Raking those same fingers through my own, short hair speckled with enough strands of silver to make me feel like an old man who'd done something dirty, I lowered it to brush my palm over the back of her head.

"Wake up, sweetheart. We've—" We've what? Got to run and hide before I get you tarnished with a brush that sticks? No matter how I phrased that one in my head it wasn't going to go down well. I cleared my throat. "We have work to do."

She stirred on my chest. Fine-boned hands that bore their own callouses pressed to my shoulders and she pushed herself up. That sapphire gaze slammed into me and would have knocked me square on my ass if I hadn't already been lying beneath her already.

"You're still here." Her soft whisper tinged with—was that hope?—brushed my ears and left me slightly breathless.

I crossed my arms behind my head and stared at her. If I touched her, there was no chance in hell we were leaving the truck any time soon. "Is there a reason I shouldn't still be here?" The words came out too-gruff. I repressed the wince that wanted to twist my features, and I refused to give her anything she could use as self-sabotaging ammunition. "Anyway, the bed's comfy. No bugs. Woke up with this stunner, though." Despite my intentions, I untangled my hands from their death grip behind my head and trailed my fingers along her cheek.

She stared at me, her eyes wide, lips parted. The pink tip of her tongue flicked out to whet her still-swollen bottom lip, and I was done.

A deep groan left my mouth as I pulled her up my body, both hands wrapped around her waist.

She squeaked a seriously cute little sound I'd have to make her repeat later on. Soft lips molded to mine in a sweet kiss that sent shocks of desire straight to my cock. I laced my hands in her hair and crashed my mouth to hers. Any thought of a languid lovemaking session dissipated in a second. I found her delightfully curved ass with one palm and ground her against me.

"Hell, sweetheart. I'm a raging hormonal teen with you," I ground out the words. My voice ended in a rasp as I pulled her back to me.

She nodded, her words lost in kisses that shifted from passionate to delirious. Her left leg fell open, knees pressed either side of my hips and she glided her soaked cleft along the painfully hard ridge of my cock.

I broke the kiss, sucking cold morning air into my lungs. Two fingers found my lips, and she gave them a little tap.

"Uh uh. You need to pay attention, Mister Foreman. Because how things run here might not be how you're used to things happening."

Mischief sparkled in her eyes, fine lines creasing the corners. She gave me a slow, sexy as sin smile and rubbed her body along mine like a kitten.

"Fuck, Nat." I gripped her hips tight, but couldn't bear to halt the glide of her flesh over mine.

"I thought you wanted to see?"

I blinked, my hands falling away. "What?"

"Last night. Remember?" She dipped her chin. Dark waves tumbled forward over her face to create a curtain that draped over my chest. She twisted, leaning over me to extract something from a small, built in drawer, and spun on my hips so she was facing the other way.

A rustling noise filled the cabin while I stared at her plump ass, just perfect for squeezing. Some perverse part of me needed to see my handprint embedded in her pale flesh. I slapped one side, then the other. She arched, a low moan filling the cab.

I couldn't have cared less if the whole damn town heard us fucking. What we did now was just me and her, and anyone else could go straight to hell.

Pretty sure that wasn't where we were headed.

Light fingernails scraped over my balls which tightened instantly. My cock bobbed against her hand, which received the same treatment. She began to jack me as she had the night before, leaning down to swipe her tongue my entire length.

My head fell back to the pillow, though I caught her ass and squeezed her heated skin, stretching her open. I propped myself onto my elbows, tracing my thumbs over her deep pink slicked skin. Her pussy lips were coated with her arousal, and swollen with need.

Her tongue wrapped around my cock. She slid her mouth up and down my length, pausing at the tip to suckle like she was French kissing it. Her lips released me from their tormenting prison, and she rolled the rubber over my length.

A quick glance over her shoulder as she raised herself and positioned me told me this one would work in her favor.

I was completely fine with that.

Her thighs trembled as she paused over me, squeezing my hips already. Heat emanated onto my cock. I rubbed my fingers over her, sliding two inside as she straightened over me. Wet flesh tightened around my fingers, milking gently. I moaned at the sensation. Shoving myself up from the mattress, I pulled my fingers out of her and pressed them to her lips, my arm around her chest arched her back against me. She licked and sucked my fingers one by one, her tongue tracing over my knuckles in a sexy as sin gesture.

"Christ, Nat. I can barely think around you."

My fingers left her mouth with a distinct pop. "Then stop stalling, Mister Foreman."

She kissed my fingers, pushing my hand away and began her slow descent over my cock. Warmth encompassed me, her inner muscles already working, undulating in the same rhythm as her hips.

I leaned back, letting the weight of her globes fill my palms, and split her apart enough to watch myself enter her.

That sight alone nearly ended me on the spot.

Inhaling long breaths through my nose, I let her move, a voyeur at my own rodeo. Her hips curved violently at the waist as she moved over me.

"Enjoying the show, Jude?" Her breathless voice held a note of amusement.

A large part of me needed to grab her hips and slam her down on me, but I was too wrapped up in enjoying what she gave me as a morning treat. "Damn right."

I thrust my hips up a little, needing to take something on my own terms, and was pleased at the quaver that wobbled the end of her single word.

"Good."

She rose and fell in a rhythm all of her own. Her hair would have covered my view but she kept it tucked over her shoulder, giving me a front row seat. She ground forward, flicking my balls with her fingertips, scratching her nails along the insides of my thighs.

I gritted my teeth, but everything she did brought me to the precipice and kept me there, relentless. "Nat, I—"

"Help me." She caught my hands, lifting them off her ass to close them around her hips and pushed down. Hard. "I need—"

"I got you, girl." I pushed down on her hips, over and over, bucking my own up to stroke into her at a furious rate.

Her nails dug into my hands. Sweat and arousal slicked my thighs, coating my balls with her need.

"Jude," she whispered. "Harder."

I relaxed my tenuous hold on my control, unable to hold back when she begged so damn pretty. Her body slapped against mine, her cries muffled behind her fist. I shoved myself back to sitting, letting her straddle me and drove deeper. My arm wound my tight around her chest, pulling her back against me. The heat of her warmed my already flushed skin.

My tongue flicked out, and I licked the sweat that beaded her cheek. "Come for me, sweetheart."

She arched in my tight hold, and her tight walls clamped down on me, pulsing as her orgasm slammed into her. Heat flooded me, gushing onto my thighs. My own pleasure became a one way, unstoppable chase. Nat muffled her scream behind the back of her hand. I yanked it free and turned her head to cover her mouth with mine as my own pleasure erupted, swallowing her cries to savor every night.

By the time she stopped screaming, we were a breathless tangle of limbs stretched across her mattress.

I doubted she'd ever get the smell of us out of her bed.

CHAPTER 5

I stared at the truck load of elk headed for Red Hart and shook my head. Travis was going to shoot me on sight, if not run me off his land but...well. If he wanted the job done differently, then he could come down and do it his own damn self.

The rest of the morning had gone differently than I'd expected. When we emerged from the truck—together, I wasn't going to let her walk the gauntlet alone—there were no sideways glances or catcalls, nothing that made either of us embarrassed. The only thing out of place, once Nat had convinced that Red Hart's best future option in diversifying meant running elk over cattle, was Gage. The ex-soldier loitered across the emptying saleyards as the rest of the buyers and sellers loaded their stock and toddled off to their part of the state and beyond.

"Are you going to be right getting out of here? It's muddy as a pile of pigs in sh—ah, slop." I covered the slip poorly, and tried not to wince.

Natalie laughed at me. "It's fine, Jude. I'm a big girl, and I've heard a whole lot worse. Promise." She gave me a slow, sexy as hell wink. The corners of her lips turned up in a wicked smile.

My own lips mirrored hers. I wound my arm around her waist and pulled her into my hip. "That doesn't mean I have to drop my manners around you." I leaned forward to brush my lisp against her ear. "Though I might when I fuck you later tonight."

A delicious shiver worked its way along her arms, and she pressed her body fully against mine. "Okay."

"That was easy."

"Did you just call me easy?" She faked outrage.

I thought she faked it.

A tall takeaway coffee cup was pressed into my hand.

"Thought you might need it." Gage gave me a roguish wink, and I recalled the man had been military.

"What's that?" I took a sip. It wasn't too bad, but I still missed Eve's coffee machine.

"Cause the whole yard could hear you two going at it. Pulled an all nighter, huh? Or did you need to take a rest in the middle, old man?" His face was straight, but his crinkled gaze held more mischief than a truckload of elk.

Natalie giggled.

I choked on my coffee.

Natalie held out her hand. I passed my takeaway cup to her and swiped the back of my hand across my mouth. When I'd cleaned up, I raised my gaze and locked onto Gage's smirking face. "You know that job I mentioned?"

His eyes lit up.

Good. Asshole.

"Don't worry about it." I collected my cup and spun on my heel. I wasn't usually such a bastard, but this morning brought out the worst of me. Maybe it was having to crawl out of bed when all I wanted was to stay right where I'd started.

That pulled me up short. I couldn't remember the last time I hadn't wanted to get out of bed.

Ever.

Gage spluttered behind me, and Natalie sent me a reproachful look.

A snort made it past clenched teeth. I waved a hand and managed to take a real sip of coffee, imbibing it through the right hole in my face. "All right. Stop."

Gage's mumbling apologies ceased, though the humor in his gaze had narrowed to something wary.

My stomach took a dive at the thought of screwing up the camaraderie I'd developed with the man, but if he was going to work at Red Hart, then I needed to know he wasn't going to pull pranks on me all day. Pull pranks on Trav on the other hand...the corner of my mouth lifted, unbidden.

"You want to work a job on a deer farm? Cause I'm not taking cattle back with me." I nodded to Nat's second big white truck packed with elk. Her cattle truck had left earlier in the morning to avoid cross contamination.

"I can do that." Gage still sounded cautious, though he rocked forward a little.

"Good." I said it, though I didn't feel it. Still, that was the job, even if it was a lonely one. It wasn't like I hadn't lived the life for long enough. "We have rules. You work hard, we pay good and we feed well. Decent living quarters, but it is a bunkhouse, and it can get rowdy. We have a no flirting policy around the house. Eve and Travis own the land, and it's a damn good farm. Eve is off limits. To everyone," I added at his raised eyebrow.

Natalie shifted beside me.

"Married couple? Doesn't seem much to worry about." Gage wiggled his other eyebrow.

"That's a talent," Natalie commented.

"They're twins. Eve has a man, he's just...not around." I pressed my lips together.

If Eve wanted anyone to know what was happening between her and Archer, then she could tell them herself. Hell, it had been several months since he'd left. I still didn't know what was going on and I lived in Eve's back pocket most of the time.

"Noted. So, can I come with you?"

"Got a truck?" I canted my head. "'Cause the seat in mine's taken."

"I'll ride with Bitty John there." Gage pointed to the young kid ready in the driver's seat of Nat's truck.

His young face flushed as his gaze flicked over Gage.

My gaze narrowed. Maybe I needed to broaden the meaning of Red Hart's no flirting policy.

"Johnny will be good company for you," Natalie said reprovingly.

Gage held her gaze for a moment, almost challenging, though heat rose in his cheeks.

There was a story there, and I got the feeling he wouldn't give it up with ease.

"All right, guess we have a convoy going."

Nat linked her arm through mine and raised her coffee. "Road trip!"

Gage laughed, his gaze lingering on her.

My fake smile managed to stay on my face until we got to my truck. Then, despite my earlier misgivings, I kissed her stupid in front of everyone.

The road was blessedly clear of traffic, and the hours went fast. Soon we were headed past White Cap, the tiny town at the bottom of the mountain range. Natalie emerged from Beanies, our local coffee haunt, though the town was a good two hour drive from Red Hart.

Frigid air whipped Natalie's auburn hair around her face in a fiery halo of wild locks. She dashed across the road, left her coffee on my truck roof and slid her arms around my waist. Icy fingers crept beneath my layers, and I let out a yelp.

"Good thing the boys aren't here to listen to you scream like a girl." Her blue eyes pooled with mischief.

"I've got my hands full between you and those two, haven't I?" I rubbed the back of my neck, nodding to where her truck had already disappeared up the range. Gage and Johnny's load was heavier. The road was winding as hell, and there was a damn fine chance we would catch them up before they hit Red Hart's drive. "Ready to go?"

"Looking forward to a little more time with you before I have to work again." Her smile dimmed a little.

I slipped my fingers into her hair, holding her close as I studied her. "What do you mean?"

She shrugged, twisting, but I held her tight.

Finally, she let out a light breath and stopped fighting me. "When we reach Red Hart, my time won't be with you for a bit.

Maybe at all." She sucked her bottom lip between her lips.

I hardened instantly and fought the need to drive somewhere private and take her over the hood of my truck. That thought did absolutely nothing to relieve the pressure building in the front of my jeans.

"Sure you will," I strived for a casual tone. Her skin was soft beneath my thumb, and I grazed it over her cheek. "We'll unpack the stock, work out where they're going, set up feed. Do we need extra feed?"

"No," Natalie sighed, nuzzling into my touch.

My pain became an ache, but I got the impression she wasn't answering my question. "No?"

"I mean, as soon as I get there I need to sell the animals to Travis and...Eve." She paused, her gaze connecting with mine.

I fell fast and hard and never hit the ground. Cold air brushed my lips, stealing the warmth of her body pressed to mine. I sucked in a lungful, grateful for the frigid wake up call.

My lips twisted as I looked down at her. "That's the third time you've mentioned her name since I met you, you know," I murmured, turning small circles on the back of her neck with my thumb.

An utterly delicious shiver I hoped had nothing to do with the cold rippled over her. "It is?" she managed.

I nodded. "Yeah. And I'm pretty sure I saw a green-eyed monster looking back at me a moment ago."

Natalie yanked her head out of my hold, her palms pressed flat to my stomach. "Is that so?"

"Mhhm." I caught her wrists and gently drew her hands to my lips. She curled them into tight fists, but I kissed each knuckle anyway. "You have nothing to worry about. Eve has been a sister to me since I was fourteen. And I'm not into incest."

Natalie's nose twitched, and her gaze narrowed. "If you say so." She pushed away from me in a swirl of burnt cinnamon curls. Her coffee cup disappeared from the top of my truck. She climbed into the passenger seat as I walked around the front, fiddling one-handed with her seatbelt and making a hell of a fuss about the thing.

I closed my hands over hers, and her jerky movements stilled. "Nat."

"Yes?" Her head stayed down.

I grazed a knuckle under her cheek, and she let me tilt her chin up to meet my gaze. "I don't want anyone but you. And I won't abandon you at Red Hart. I promise." I leaned forward to brush my mouth over hers in a gentle kiss.

Then her lips opened, and I pulled her hard into my chest. A groan ripped free from my throat, and a tiny mewl echoed it. All rational thought left my head as she wound her arms around my neck, lifting up against me.

Five minutes later, I finally started the truck, my lips still tingling from our make out session.

White Cap disappeared behind a mountain before Natalie emerged from the other side of her coffee cup. A soft sigh filled the cab, so like the ones of this morning—hell, had it only been this morning?—and my arousal peaked once more.

"That good, huh?" My voice came out gruff, but there was damn near nothing I could do about that without giving myself away.

Hell, I'd only known her for a day or two, though known was probably pushing it.

"Mhmm." Natalie's mischievous gaze slanted sideways at me.

My fingers choked the steering wheel. "Why don't you tell me about yourself?"

Her laughter filled the cab of my truck. When her giggles subsided, and she had snorted into the remnants of her coffee, she offered me a crooked smile. "You really are awkward, aren't you?"

The steering wheel squeaked beneath my fingers. "I'm fine to travel in silence." I stared at the road, the world narrowing into two black lanes I knew would soon turn to dirt.

"Oh, Jude." Natalie's fingers curled around my knee, sliding up the denim. She scooted across the edge of her seat and leaned into my shoulder. "I'm sorry. You're just such an easy target." She smiled at me sheepishly, her head rested against my shoulder.

The warmth was a comfortable weight, and her fingers tracing patterns on the inside of my thigh were doing crazy things to my head.

"It's fine," I said again. Shifting did nothing and I was unable to rid myself of the stiff tone that spread to my spine until I sat rigid and unyielding in the driver's seat. "I'm not a social person."

"You've done fine until right now," she murmured.

"Well, I haven't had you yanking my chain until just now. Is it going to be a regular thing?"

"I love your sense of humor."

I snorted. "I think we just proved you don't." Or maybe that she shouldn't.

"Mhhm. You're fun."

I clenched my teeth and pressed my foot on the gas a touch harder.

Natalie gave me a good ten second's grace. "I grew up in the US, in South Carolina. Graduated law school, went to a rodeo with some friends on summer break for giggles. I discovered I liked cowboys, married one and then found out he was Canadian." She shook her head, bemusement lacing her voice as she lounged against me.

I slept with a married woman?

The thought didn't sit well with me. I glanced down at her fingers, but there wasn't even a tan line to show where a wedding ring should have sat.

"I'm a widow. I wouldn't do that, Jude. Not ever." Her tone held more than a touch of reproach.

I winced. "I'm— shit. I'm sorry." I pressed my lips into a tight line.

"It's okay. I probably should have warned you."

Maybe, but I wasn't about to say it. "So, Canada. I bet that was a surprise. You didn't think to ask?" I unwrapped one hand from the steering wheel and covered hers where it rested on my thigh.

She wound her fingers through mine and snuggled deeper against my side. "His parents lived in the south. His accent was...well, a bit all over the place, but I figured as a rider on a rodeo circuit, he must have become a bit of a mutt. So anyway," she poked my side, "I moved to Canada. Roger bought land, and we built the business from the ground up. He knew ranching, I knew law and a little bit of business. It worked out well, for a time." Fondness slipped into her voice. Natalie stopped speaking.

I might have thought she was finished, but her fingers clawed into my hand. Breath whooshed from my lungs. I gave a gentle squeeze back, then disengaged my hand from hers. She made the tiniest sound of protest, half cut off.

"It's okay, sweetheart." I slipped my arm around her shoulders, pulling her tight to my side. "Tell me what happened?"

It was a question, not a demand. No woman should have to speak about a tragedy like that for someone she'd obviously loved.

"Roger, he— Cancer." Her teeth closed with an audible clack.

"Fuck. That's a mess." I tightened my hold on her.

She made another soft sound, a long breath that left her slumped against me. "It took eighteen months. We flew for treatments, we drove for treatments. It took me less than a month to recognize I couldn't work the land alone, and so I started hiring. I ran the business side more. By the time Roger was gone, the place was an automaton. I just lived there. And when he was gone—"

I swallowed hard and waited, but she didn't say anything more.

"You didn't have anything to fill your hours, huh?"

She gave me a jerky nod and swiped the back of her hand across her eyes. "My sob story. Also, I love books and I hate waste. Recycle anything I can. So. Tell me something about you."

"I hate crowds."

"I got that."

"With a passion."

"That too. Tell me something I don't know, Jude. Something that makes you you."

I ran my mind over my years at Red Hart. It took me all of a minute to work out where to start. "The first day I was at Red Hart, I was punched in the nose by my best friend. I turned up at Travis' doorstep when I was fourteen, frozen stiff, riding up the mountain on the back of a hay bale because my shitty old rig died halfway across the country. The guy who drove half a dozen of us up didn't have enough seats so we climbed into the bed. Trav let me into the house, told the rest of the boys to head down to the bunk house and clean up. He—I don't know, he saw a kid his age, maybe. He let me shower, and I might have walked in on his twin sister in the nude."

"I bet that went down well."

"He damn near broke my nose and told me never to come into the house again. Eve over rode him and told me I was on kitchen prep for however long it took Trav to forgive me." I grinned. "I still sleep in the bunkhouse."

"Did he ever forgive you?"

"I doubt it. You should ask him."

"I'm not very good with family."

"They aren't my family."

"Sounds like they are to me."

"Maybe." I supposed she was right. I hadn't seen my blood relations in nearly twenty years, and I'd been at Red Hart almost that long. "We had a few...tragedies recently." A glance in her direction revealed this wasn't news. Damn that the twin's business had spread that far afield. "Anyway, now you know my secret."

"Did you have a crush on her?"

"Eve?"

"Yeah."

"Hell, no. Admired her and looked up to a girl who was my age but could tell a cowboy to sit down, shut up and eat the food she cooked and still have him respect her at the end of the meal, even work his ass to the ground for her the next day, or week or month. It took me a whole lot longer to learn how to manage that skill for myself."

"And now you're a foreman." A speculative glint entered her eyes.

"You're not poaching me, Nat. Red Hart is my home."

"Mmhmm. You've never seen Granite Falls."

My brow knit. "You do border on Black Hill land then. Didn't you have an avalanche a bit back?"

"Damn near took out the house." She shook her head. "I told Roger not to choose a site so close, but...he wouldn't listen." A rueful smile played over her lips.

My fingers tightened around her shoulder. I relaxed them with effort. "You really loved him, didn't you?"

What in the hell are you doing? You've known her for less than forty-eight hours.

But being around Natalie wasn't like any other new acquaintance.

You don't fuck your new acquaintances.

Well, that was a simple one. Usually I met young cowboys, or older ones like Gage with a history of their own. We worked shoulder-to-shoulder over a problem, and that broke the barriers down. The only women in my life now were Eve and Rachel.

Eve may as well be my sister, and Rachel was firmly attached to Travis, no matter how much he tried to push the dark-haired vet away, albeit in a half-hearted fashion. We all knew they were sweet on each other, and Trav's ongoing leg and hip issues had only brought them closer.

"Yes, I did." Natalie tilted her head back on my shoulder, staring up at me. "You—" She cleaned her throat. "Are we close?"

I grinned, taking my eyes off the road for a moment just to focus on her. When I drew my attention back to where it should be, the top of

94

her white stock hauler was visible over the next rise.

"Were you going to ask if we were there yet?"

"Mhmmmm." She shook her head.

Dark curls brushed the back of my hand, eliciting a fresh, pine forest scent that went straight to my head.

"Got a whole lotta attitude going there, girl."

"If you say so."

"And you're a bit of a brat, aren't you?" I didn't need to look down at her to see the way her eyes widened in faux innocence.

"How could you suggest such a thing?" Her fingers squeezed my thigh, a little higher than they had been before.

"Could it be because you're used to having things your own way?"

"Maybe?" We sped over the same rise her truck had disappeared behind. The world behind us dropped away, and she gasped.

I hid a smile behind cold coffee dregs, driving with my knees while I took a sip.

Mountains rose on either side of the road in a valley of green filtering out to a plateau of gold. Red Hart's winding drive trundled through a series of hillocks. The big house wasn't visible from the road, but the peak that rose behind it was, the late afternoon sunlight slanting across its lush slopes in an array of pinks and oranges.

"It's like the mountain is blushing," Natalie whispered.

"You don't usually come in on this road?" You don't see this from your side of the mountain? She had to back onto it, if she owned the land I thought she did. I snuck a sideways glance at her.

"I've never been this way. We use the customs crossing to the west."

"Long way around."

"Maybe, but it's safer with a truck full of stock. Nowhere near as pretty, though."

"Fair enough." I pulled up to the drive.

Gage held the gate open and waved us through. Red Hart's giant black and red sign emblazoned with the fiery antlers Eve plastered on everything stood tall at his back.

"It's incredible. So...different." Natalie never stopped craning her neck to peer around the hills in sheer awe.

"So you've really never seen it from this side?"

"Not this view."

That's not the same thing.

I nodded. Her evasive response niggled at me. I didn't know why, but it did. I stopped on the other side of the gate long enough for Gage to close up. The truck rocked as he jumped onto the flatbed and gave the side a firm tap.

"Well then, welcome to Red Hart Ranch." I wound down my window to give Gage a wave to let him know we were off.

Natalie nodded, her fingers wound tight in her lap.

The words didn't taste as sweet as I'd expected. I closed my mouth and accelerated down the first hill toward the house.

CHAPTER 6

The minutes to the ranch passed in silence. Despite wanting to watch the joy wash over her face at the sight of the grand old ranch house seated at the foot of the mountain, I didn't end up looking. The ground drifted silently beneath us in a familiar path. Dust lifted in her truck's wake, not yet settled in the quiet afternoon light. Even the air stilled, pensive.

I gripped the steering wheel with whitening knuckles, wondering just what I'd brought to Red Hart's door.

After the last fiasco that left us two family members short, I wasn't keen for any more drama. This was my home, and it had always been a safe place…until recently.

"It's beautiful. Are you glad to be home?" Natalie nestled against my side.

I shrugged, and unwound my arm from her shoulders under the pretense of changing gears, though I'd done it southpaw just fine a moment ago.

Natalie shifted beside me, her body twisting. "Jude?"

"Yeah."

The drive opened out into a wide yard. The barn I'd spent weeks painting after Travis' accident sat to one side, just off center, and opposite the big house. Nat's truck was parked dead in the middle, as though the poor kid had been overwhelmed by the massive space and unsure what to do next.

"Johnny," Natalie muttered in reproach beneath her breath.

"'S'all right. I got it." Gage thumped my window with his closed fist and jogged to the truck. He pulled open the door and jumped into the driver's seat.

A chuckle escaped my throat. I could only imagine how the kid felt. Being that young was too many years ago to look back on, and too painful to boot.

"It's good to hear you laugh." Natalie swiveled around, wrapped her hands in my shirt and pulled me down to kiss her.

My lips grazed over hers, soft and tender before her hands wrapped around my neck. She arched up against me, seeking the pressure she needed. A groan at the thought of her grinding her hips against my groin ripped through my mind. My arms folded around her tight, crushing her to me.

Her tongue brushed against mine and her kiss faltered, but I was too far gone to let her go. I slanted my mouth over hers, taking, and tasting. Savoring her. Tiny cries emanated from the base of her throat. I pulled back before I had her right there, my chest heaving.

A heavy knock on the driver's window to my truck left me nearly wetting myself. I twisted to glare over my shoulder. Travis glared back at me, the usual laugh lines around his mouth absent.

"Fuck." I turned back to Nat and grazed my thumb over her cheek. "Guess it's time for that work aspect of the day, huh?"

Dark blue eyes caught mine and held. "I guess so." Her lips tightened, and she squeezed my thigh.

I let out a slow sigh and motioned back over my shoulder so I wouldn't collide with Travis on his crutches and flicked my thumb over the door latch.

Natalie gave me a small, reassuring smile over her shoulder, though her gaze flicked up to focus behind me for an instant. I read the uncertainty there and wondered if it was me or the job that worried her more. She'd seemed concerned about the sale she'd made to me, but I'd back my own decision—and her—one hundred percent.

Maybe she'd had some shitty experiences with foremen buying for their ranches? Not that there was any point worrying about it. We were here now, and we had a job to do. Both of us. I shrugged it off and stepped out of my truck.

"You're back." Trav had propped himself up with one crutch a few feet away.

I pushed my hat on and shoved my hands into my jean pockets. "It's good to be home."

"Is it? You seem to have found a replacement for us already." Trav's gaze tracked action behind me.

It didn't take a genius to work out it was Natalie, as Gage and Johnny were already out of the truck. Their debate over what to do drew my attention, but I raised a hand palm out, and the distraction ceased.

My eyes narrowed.

Was Trav jealous of Natalie? Granted I hadn't had more than a few flings ever, really, preferring to work and enjoyed my time on the land and away from everyone. Now I come home and suddenly I was as out of place on the land as I had been on it.

A confidence knocker there, for sure.

"You asked me to get stock. I got you stock. Let me unpack it. I think Ms Crossman has information you'll need." My teeth clacked together on the last word. I leveled my best friend a hard stare, as though trying to break through his hard fascade, but the fucker was as stubborn as me at the best of times. "Good to see you up and around." I gave him a nod, no more than a jerk of my head, and took a step toward the truck, my mind already on what to do with the stock and where to house them.

"Jude." Trav's voice strained as he stepped forward and halted. His face whitened, and he grabbed his crutch in hands as pale as his face.

"Fuck," I cursed myself. The short distance felt long as I closed it and shoved one shoulder beneath his arm, detaching the crutch from his side and taking his weight. "You really are an—"

"Asshole. Yeah, you tell me all the time."

"Doesn't change anything though, does it?" A quick grin stretched my lips.

Trav mirrored my smile. "Might. Keep trying."

"Fuck off."

We grinned at each other and the animosity that had strained the air between us for too long a moment dissipated in an instant.

I helped Trav to the short flight of stairs that led to the big house and managed to get him onto the veranda. He stopped there, cuddling a post, and leaned his body weight against the railing.

When I spun on my heel to help unload the truck, his hand fell on my shoulder. His tight grip stopped me.

"Jude?"

"Yeah?"

"Why are there elk in my yard?"

My lips curved in a small smile as I looked back at him in a dare me, fucker look. "Because they are the diverse future of Red Hart Ranch."

I clattered down the steps, marking the dirt I'd left there without removing my boots to clean off later, and was halfway to the truck when Trav's grumble reached my ears.

"That had better not be a metaphor. I'm not good with those."

I wasn't, either. Both of us were straight shooters, said what we needed, did the job and stayed home. Usually. I opened my mouth to cuss him for the barb, but Natalie appeared around the edge of the truck, and my step slowed.

Hers didn't. Natalie had a power stride going that propelled her forward with the same energy she'd had when I first met her in the saleyards. She gave me a board and obvious wink as she passed, but her attention was fully engaged with the ranch owner behind me.

"Jude may not be good with metaphors, but I sure am." Her introduction left me with a broad grin as I made it to the back of the truck and outlined my plan to Johnny and Gage.

Even if she had left me as a scapegoat.

Four long hours later, I'd learned how much it hurts when a pregnant elk kicks you in the balls. Gage fell down laughing, rolling in the dirt in his hilarity.

"Thanks," I rasped dryly. "You're a real help here."

"Glad to be of assistance." He rolled swiftly to his feet in a fluid, practiced moment. His hat banged against his thigh, eliciting a decent puff of dust and grit before he angled it on his head with one hand, walking toward me all the time.

Johnny stood beside me, his mouth hanging open in an obvious display of hero worship. Gage chucked the kid under his chin and gave him a saucy wink.

I had a feeling my jaw own wasn't too far behind and covered the uncomfortable emotion with a fake cough I hid behind my tight fist. "Save it for the showgirls, Fred Astaire."

"All battleground tactics, my friend." Gage clapped his hand on my shoulder, presenting his back to Johnny. His grip tightened, and I looked up into eyes filled with shadows that came with a knowledge of things a man should never have to understand.

Mine had been filled with something similar when I arrived at Red Hart after escaping my self-destructing childhood home.

"Note made not to tackle you anytime soon." I rubbed the back of my neck with a hot hand and exchanged an awed glance with Johnny.

Who the hell had I brought to Red Hart, and what the hell was I going to do with him?

"You ready to head up to the house? I'll bet Eve made something decent for dinner." My stomach growled as though saying their words had incited my hunger, though it roiled beneath my body's needs for a very different reason.

I'd been home half a day, and I hadn't even gone to see her. I shook my head, and swiped the back of my hand over my mouth, leaving a trail of grime I'd have to wash off before I saw her. No doubt she'd kick my ass when I got in.

Maybe Natalie too.

My heart stalled at the thought of both of them together. Hell, would they have gotten along? Nat had seemed so hesitant about the thought of Eve. What did she think of her in person? I hadn't even considered Eve's thoughts, though I doubted she would take any issue with Nat. She dealt with Rachel in the house just fine.

Usually, the only person she took issue with was her twin and that was just sibling stuff.

Not that I'd know, but I had always assumed. That had probably started in my head around the time they both took it on themselves to adopt me, or maybe it was the other way around.

Johnny looked at me curiously from under a very clean hat that was at least two sizes too big for him.

My phone buzzed in my pocket. I checked the screen then eyeballed Johnny. "Nat's got you a bed in the bunkhouse. Fair warning, these assholes all snore."

He nodded silently, his gaze flicking back at the trucks winding their way back to the house.

I huffed a breath as I pulled the gate to the elk's new paddock closed, eyeballing the starter herd. The pregnant female stood on her own, though the rest clustered together, nibbling at the supplement feed Nat had insisted on gifting us.

"Come on, kid. We've got a bit of a drive back. I'll tell you a story."

I hoisted myself up into the truck beside Gage. We headed back to the house beneath a purple haze as twilight fell over the land.

A soft glow emanating from the house washed over the yard by the time we made it up to dinner. I'd insisted we all wash up at the bunkhouse and had taken the time to show the boys where they would be sleeping. A few other seasonal ranch hands filtered in, grimy, yawning and hungry.

"Damn." Gage whistled. He kicked his boots off at the door and peered into Red Hart's enormous, open plan living area. "This place must be worth a few million."

"Around forty or so, last time someone tried to sell the idea of moving to the city to Eve. Trav strung the real estate agent along for a bit, just for giggles. He can be a little bitch when he's in the mood." I took my hat off, poised to hang it on its peg, but the damn thing was taken. I sorted hats and jackets around until they were in an order I could understand and put mine where it belonged. Nat's jacket hung on a peg closer to the door.

I brushed my knuckles over the sleeve, and the scent of mountains and icy air hit me in a wave that removed the scent of whatever Eve had cooked through the ranch house's big double doors.

Gage's shoulder bashed against mine. "Man, you got it bad."

I grunted my agreement. The man was right. I couldn't go five minutes without thinking about her. Not really watching where I was going, engrossed in a vague day dream of what I'd do to Nat when we made it to the guest bedroom for the night and ran straight into Gage's back.

"The fu—" A shadow loomed between Gage and the door.

I cut my words off in a clack of teeth and took a discreet step back.

"Where are you going? I might need you to cover my ass," Gage hissed over his shoulder, though his easy grin belied the tension in his words.

"Gage, this is Travis Beaumont. Owner of Red Hart Ranch and the man you'll be working for this summer, or however long you last."

"However long I last?" Gage's voice rose, tinged with incredulity.

"It's tougher out here than you might think. We try to keep it social, but...we're a damn long way from anywhere. Trav, this is Gage. Ex-soldier, hard worker. Got a bit of a dancer in him, too."

"Good. I'll dress you up in a skirt and you can entertain the troops, Twinkle Toes."

Gage laughed, a relaxed sound that held a harsh, grating edge at the end, as though something had damaged his voice at some point. He slapped Travis' arm, stepping around the taller man with no indication he was intimidated at all.

Knowing what I did about the slightly older man, he probably wasn't.

"Just call me Cap."

Trav turned back to me with a hard stare. "The fuck have you brought back to my ranch, man?"

I shrugged. "Dunno. But it's your damn fault for sending me off the land." I clipped his jaw with a light fist.

Trav lunged forward to grapple me. Air hissed between his teeth, and he grabbed for the door frame. I pushed him back into the position where he had been leaning against the wall—for support, I realized belatedly—and propped him up.

Travis grumbled under his breath as I aimed him toward the leather armchairs that surrounded a lit fire. It might not be winter any more, but that didn't mean the nights got much warmer. Not for a few more weeks, in any case.

"No. I want to have dinner with everyone else." He winced as I took his full weight across my shoulders, lowering his legs first onto the three-seater. The thing was just long enough that his legs bumped the opposite end.

"Sit down and shut up, old man. I'll get your dinner."

"I should be at the table with the boys. With Eve," he added as I jammed a pillow under his lower back. "My father would have."

113

"Your father—" I closed my eyes, and inhaled a long breath. "Len sat at the head of the table most nights, but I remember plenty when he wasn't there."

"Yeah? Apart from when he was dying?" Trav rasped the words in a harsh growl.

I cleared my face of any wince, unwilling to let him rant and have his pity party. "Do you know those times? Once when Eve broke up with her first boyfriend. She was in tears for days. No one could settle her. So your father took her out for the night, up onto the mountain. They walked in with packs on their backs. Found some old ranger station up there that hadn't been used in an age. Your father—Trav, he didn't listen to the grumbles the hands made, and Betty never said a word. Mid-summer, and they came back early the next day. Both of them were working before anyone else got up, and Eve never cried another tear over that little dick."

Trav stopped bitching and stared hard at me. "Damn. There's a good reason you don't talk so much." The corner of his lip quirked. "Yeah, I remember that. I remember you punched the kid and broke his nose the next time you saw him."

"Some one had to." I shrugged it off. "The other time your father wasn't at that table was because of you."

"Yeah."

"You remember?"

"I don't want to talk about it."

I pressed my palms to my knees and rose out of my crouch. "You should. Len was a good man and a good rancher. But you know something, Trav? Get your head out of tradition, and out of your ass, and I reckon you can be a better one."

I turned away from my best friend, hoping to God above that I'd said the right thing, and headed to the table for a plate.

By the time I'd sorted Travis and sat down to my own food the long table was empty except for a pair of varying shades of reddish-brown heads bent together, chattering away at the other end. Eve and Nat. I had no idea how similar they were, until I saw them sitting opposite each other. Both with long dark wavy hair, though Natalie's was a little darker, chocolate with a hint of auburn, where Eve's curls sported garnet glints in the firelight. They both wore dark, slim jeans and boots, coupled with long sleeved cotton shirts. Natalie's was striped blue and white, Eve's was red.

I shook my head and dug into the steak and mash Eve had left heaped on a plate for me. I hadn't had a chance to speak to her before she was whisked away for something else, and the closest I'd gotten to Natalie was to wave at her from the other end of the table.

Even Gage had dipped his head to kiss her cheek and bid her good night, though I noted how his gaze lingered on Eve. Trav would notice too, then the man would be out of a job. I made a mental note to speak to him about house rules in the morning, before Trav ripped him a new one for checking out his sister, injured or not.

 CHAPTER 7

My belly filled too fast. I wrapped my roast beef leftovers in foil and stowed them in the side of the fridge for lunch the next day. I wanted to speak to Natalie and see if we could work out if she bordered on our land at all, and get her opinion on a few ideas I had for our new part of the herd.

And, of course, she'd leave and that would be the end of seeing her again.

She's one property away.

Yes, but there was a mountain in the way, for Christ's sake.

A small hand pressed against my back. I sighed and turned. "I'm so sorry I haven't had a chance to— Eve." I closed my mouth as I stared at her, taking in the dark circles under her eyes, the sallow skin I haven't noted before. Had she been like that for long? Since before I left to get stock? Maybe I was seeing her for the first time with fresh eyes simply because I hadn't been around for a few days. "Are you okay?"

"Just tired." She offered me a small smile, then yawned widely. Eve clapped her hand over her mouth and blinked at me above it.

I laughed and pulled her into a hug. "I'm sorry. I thought you were—"

"Natalie. Mhmm. I noticed." Eve hung onto me tight, her fine arms wrapped around my shoulders.

"Yeah. That." I shrugged off the feeling that she was watching me, even though I couldn't see her eyes. I held her at arm's length, inspecting her. Exhausted eyes stared at me from a ghost of a woman. The last few months had been hard, but the thought that I had been blind to her wasting away, much as her mother had in her last weeks after Len had passed, ruined me. "Tell me what you need."

"To rewind a year? Or two?" Eve uttered a short, barking laugh and swept her hair back from her face. "Let me clean up, Jude. I need some quiet. If you can help Trav up to his bed, then you can spend time however you like with Natalie." She pulled away from me, heading toward the table again, then looked over her shoulder. "She seems nice."

I expected something more jovial from Eve, but her trademark blazing smile was absent, along with the elbow I expected at my ribs. Instead, seeing her so morose was a dagger between them.

"You sure you're okay?"

She shrugged. "I'm...alone."

Breath whooshed from my chest in a giant suckerpunch. I wound my arms around her tight, pulling her into me the way I had done countless times, more so in the last months. "You're not alone. Trav's here."

"Is he?" Eve pushed my chin back and raised glittering eyes to meet mine. "Trav isn't interested in the ranch any more. This— it's taken its toll, Jude. And I don't know how long I can keep paying that."

"Fine," I agreed, pushing the churning in my gut lower. "Trav's...well. He's always been a bit odd, huh? But I'm back, and I'm not going anywhere. I promise." I kissed her brow.

"You can't promise me that. And you don't have to stay." She shot a quick glance at Natalie's back.

I followed her gaze with knowing eyes. "Eve, I've been here for fifteen years. This is my home. You are my home. And Trav," I added begrudgingly.

Eve smiled, a small, sad thing, but a smile nonetheless. I was taking that as a win. "Thank you."

"Have you spoken to Archer?"

Eve dropped her arms. "Not for a bit. He's— he's very busy with his case. Down south. I think."

"Can't the man use email? He'd better as hell be looking after my Eve."

Just as fast as she'd opened up, Eve shut down. "No."

Fuck me.

Every time I managed to extract my foot from my mouth, I put the other one back in there. "Hey, it's okay."

Eve shot me a warning glance. "Go have fun with your girl."

"She's not my girl." The words fell out of my mouth in a practiced, automatic response. I cringed and waited for the slap that would follow.

Eve put her hands on her hips. "Well. She doesn't know that. And I don't need to give you a walloping, because that girl will do it for me."

"I sure hope so." I gave Eve a dopey grin that probably conveyed more than she was looking for.
She pushed both hands into my chest, shooing me off.

I rotated on my heel to take in the room. To my greatest surprise, Natalie sat talking with Travis. A tumbler of whiskey balanced in her palm, a matching one in his.

I might have to worry about Gage, but Natalie was getting on with everyone just fine.

She chatted animatedly, her arms moving with whatever story she told. I stood in the middle of the open living area between the armchairs and the long table, and let the peace I'd always found at Red Hart sink over me.

Which lasted as long as a full three seconds until Natalie looked up and caught my gaze with her fathomless one. A wicked smile curved her lips at the corners, and her eyes sparkled with their own private galaxy.

For the second time, I fell.

Maybe it was being home again, back in a place I was secure, and safe.

Or maybe it was because of her.

Either way, I was in a hell of a lot of trouble.

Travis jerked his head to follow her line of sight. His eyes flicked back and forth between us, and he shook his head with a long, drawn out sigh I heard clearly from the middle of the room.

"Come on, old man. Let's get you up to bed."

"Fuck off with the old shit." Travis didn't apologize for his language in front of Nat.

I raised an eyebrow at her, but she gave me the tiniest shake of her head. Her brow furrowed, and I imagined mine matched hers. I crossed the room and came to a halt at the end of his couch, trying to work out how I was going to get a man who weighed almost as much as me in the shade up a flight and a half of stairs on my own.

Rachel usually helped me out, and now I'd seen how tired Eve was, I was loathe to ask her for anything. Had she been hefting her brother up the stairs each night alone? Had Rachel?

"How have you— oh."

I spied the pile of blankets at the same time as Natalie gestured with one hand behind her back.

"You two done being all discrete?" Trav snapped, pushing up from the sofa. His leg hit the ground, and his snark transformed into a hiss.

"Damn, boy. Let me help." I didn't bother to add please. He'd either let me help or he wouldn't.

"Old man, boy. Make up your mind—ah." Trav gripped my shoulder too tightly as I planted mine beneath his and bore his weight across my back.

"Take a step?"

"No chance in hell."

"Which room is yours?" Natalie bounced up from the sofa. "I'll make your bed up."

"Fourth on the right, at the end of the hall." Trav's room was as far from our current position as we could get, but what was a few more steps? "You ready?"

"Born for it. Torture me."

"You're on."

By the time we made it to the stairs my shoulders were aching. At the first landing, I discovered a need to pee that refused to let up. I ignored it, anyway. "All right. Bathroom, then bedroom?"

"Are you seducing me or playing nursemaid?" Trav's good leg rested on the next step, and despite our break, his breath came labored.

"I'm not pretty enough for the first."

"Now you tell me. Bathroom. Please." His voice was less than a whisper as we started up the eleven steps that may as well have been an eternity.

"Maybe you should have stayed downstairs."

"Have you slept on that damn couch?"

"Not recently."

"Then don't second guess me," Trav snapped. He squeezed his eyes shut and gripped the banister with whitened knuckles. "Sorry."

I gritted my teeth and pushed against the dual strain of physical effort versus emotional baggage. I had enough of my own, but for the time being, I'd bear Trav's, if that was what he needed. "Eleven steps. Then you hurry the fuck up because you're not the only one with needs."

"You mean the piece of ass waiting in the spare room?"

I actually bit my tongue to prevent myself from answering that one honestly. "That piece of ass is making up your bedroom, asshole."

Trav grunted, shoving his long body up one stair at a time. His weight compressed over my back muscles, and I moved with him at a slow pace. Finally, I got him through the ensuite he shared with Eve, cleaned up and into bed. His blankets had been turned back, and his crutches rested against the wall within easy reach should he wake in the middle of the night or to get up in the morning.

"Want a goodnight kiss?" I muttered.

"Nah, you got enough of the good stuff. Need a top up already?" He rolled awkwardly to one side and yanked out a foil packet and threw it at me.

I caught it by reflex, unable to push down the embarrassment that sent flames licking at my neck. "I'm not a fucking school kid. And I'm out there making sure your damn business doesn't fail while you're not capable. Remember that." I slid the condom pack into my back pocket.

Trav's eyes tracked the movement.

Go on, fucker. Say it.

Mercifully, he didn't.

Silence filled the room for a long moment, and just as I thought he was going to up the asshole factor to a whole new level, Trav spoke into the darkness. "It's too quiet here, now."

I tipped two pain killers into my hand and made sure he swallowed them. His head hit the pillow, and he let out a groan. In a few short months the man who had been my easy-going, hard-working beast friend had become the epiphany of his bed ridden old man who only got grumpier by the day.

I gripped his foot tight at the end of the bed and switched off the light as I left his room. "I know."

His door clicked shut behind me. I stepped a few feet back along the shadowed hall and stopped. Eve's door was closed, and her light was off. No light shone through the spare room at the other end of the hall either, closest to the stairs.

I was grateful for the twins not kicking Natalie and Johnny back out on their asses. We were used to randoms turning up with trucks looking for work—a final destination for most of the stragglers who came through, as there really wasn't anything beyond us, except for the border. Still, it didn't mean they had to accept everyone who turned up on their doorstep. I couldn't remember the last time either of them had said no to anyone upfront.

After last Christmas, a lot of things had changed around Red Hart, and I suspected a wariness to new hands to be a part of that.

The door at the end of the hall opened. I waited, but Natalie didn't appear. I cast a last glance at Eve's silent room and strode down the hall. My hand hit Natalie's door too hard. I caught it and closed it behind me, leaving us both in the dark.

Her hands brushed my arms. I struggled with where she stood, though my eyes adjusted faster than I expected after our first nighttime encounter together. Her silhouette blocked the light before me.

Fingertips trailed down my arms to brush by my ribs. She tugged me forward by my shirt and slipped one button open at a time.

I caught her on the third one, my hands closing over hers.

She paused beneath my touch. "No?"

Light reflected over her skin, pale beneath the high, cloudless night that promised a crisp morning. It would be a hell of a walk back to the bunkhouse, but I'd made it often enough.

Shadowed eyes surveyed me. She pressed her palms flat to my chest and pushed me back. "That's not how this works." Her lips twitched.

My cock ached in response.

Brat.

I smiled. "Good night, Natalie."

She jerked a little, her quick inhale audible. "Good night?"

"Yeah." I leaned forward to kiss her, and I knew it was a bad idea.

CHAPTER 8

Her lips were soft and warm beneath mine, and she tasted like the whiskey I'd seen her drinking earlier. Honey and fire wrapped around me, winding me into her.

I groaned against her mouth as her lips parted, granting me access. My tongue slipped inside her mouth, dancing and stroking in slow, languid movements that removed all the blood from my brain and sent it rushing south. My fingers tangled in her silken curls. I tugged her head back, angling her to deepen the kiss. Her taste, her warmth swam around me until I couldn't think.

The backs of my hands collided with the wall, the rough surface grazing my knuckles. Nat's body pinned by mine sent an overdose of power straight to my core.

I caught her hands where they were still wrapped in my shirt and raised them over her head, keeping contact with her mouth, unable to walk away. Her fingers closed around mine. She tugged a few times, but I ignored her, kissing her deeper, longer. Her body softened against mine, her hands relaxed in my grip.

Tiny moans slipped from her lips, and I swallowed them all, craving more. My body ached for hers. I pressed my knee between her thighs, using the pressure to get more of those little cries that sent my head spinning.

She broke the kiss, gasping. I trailed kisses and nips along her jaw, to the sensitive spots on her throat I'd discovered before, and used them as a weapon until she was writhing against me. Natalie tugged on my grip at her wrists, but I held firm, content to torment her for a while longer.

"What happened to 'goodnight'?" she whispered. Her head tilted back against the wall, exposing her slim, pale throat.

I used the moment to claim another, harder kiss.

"I still have to leave," I murmured against her skin, licking at the nips I left there to soothe the heightened nerves.

"Why? Stay, please. I'll—"

I lifted my head to stare into eyes I could barely see. "You'll what?"

She stared back, unspeaking.

I sighed and dipped my head to kiss her again. "Good night, Nat." My fingers unwound from around her wrists, stroking where I'd gripped her.

Her hands dropped to her sides. "No." It was the barest whisper.

"I can't stay. I—" I swore softly. "This is like a family home to me. I can't just—"

"Just what?" Her tone held a dangerous edge.

I walked the fine line between letting her have what she wanted and getting castrated on the spot. "It's like being in your parents' home

133

and having sex while they're in the next room." I cupped her cheeks, kissing her again.

She responded in kind, arching against me. "There's no one next door. I checked."

"Not enough for what I want to do to you," I promised her.

"Raincheck?" she offered. "Or we could be quiet this time?"

"I'm not sure I could be with you," I murmured against her lips, memorizing their shape.

"Please, Jude. I—"

"Tell me." I settled my weight against her body, my knees braced between her legs, my hips tight to hers. "Don't you think I don't want you, girl."

"I—" She choked on the word.

An image rose into my head of her on her knees choking on something else. I banished the vision, or tried to, and failed. Her gaze was heavy, her eyes flitting across my face, but the words didn't come.

"Are you embarrassed to ask for what you want?" I frowned and returned her searching gaze.

Her breath hitched. "Maybe. I've never—"

"Never had to?"

"Never been confident enough," she shot back.

I nodded, and pushed away from the wall, giving her space. "Fair enough."

"Jude, please."

"Please...?" I offered helpfully.

"You're an ass."

"So people keep telling me." I grinned.

Nat made a hrumphing sound I was still trying to decipher when she launched herself at me.

Her mouth found mine, her hands wrapped around my neck for balance. I stumbled back a step, seeking balance but I'd overcommitted. Her legs wrapped around my hips, and somehow the motion stabilized us for a bare second. I caught her, but sacrificed my footing to do it. The only grace was that the bed caught us when we went down.

Unwilling to let her win this round, I rolled her beneath me and caught her jaw between my fingers. My next kiss wasn't as sweet. "Damn, that attitude, girl."

"So you keep saying."

I huffed a laugh and went to work on the buttons of her shirt.

"Jude?"

Yeah?" I stopped, pausing mid-unbutton which was a whole lot harder than it should have been in the dark.

"Are you still going to leave?" The uncertainty, the utter loneliness in her voice floored me.

I desisted with the buttons, pushing us both up the bed until I could brace my body over hers. "No, Nat. I'm not going to leave you. But I could use a hand." I guided her trembling fingers to the remaining buttons on my own shirt. "Would you?"

"Okay?" Her hesitancy was out of place, and I wondered at it after the minx she'd been last night. Hell, even up to a few minutes ago.

I waited as her hands connected with bare skin beneath the thick cotton. She made short work of the rest and pushed the material back over my shoulders. I shucked it off, tossing it to the floor and stayed braced over her. "Now yours."

She froze for a long moment, and when I expected her to turf me out the door, she caught the cotton between her fingers and slid her slim shoulders out of it. A soft, low breath hit my abdomen as she reached around to unhook her bra, which joined her shirt on the floor.

The shape of her was less than a fuzzy silhouette, and I desperately needed to feel her warmth beneath my hands. I shuffled one knee forward, closing the small space between us, and grazed my palms up her ribs.

Electricity bolted through me from fingers to the tip of my cock. My groan was a perfect match for the whisper that left her lips. I drew her to me, letting her skin warm against mine, and folded my arms around her.

Natalie's arms locked around me. She tilted her head back, and I obliged her silent request in a slow kiss that sent a zing of pure pleasure through my body, every synapse awake and languid at once. She sighed softly into my mouth, and I wondered if she'd experienced the same sensation. Her fingers worked the button on my jeans and drew them over my hips, touching my bare skin beneath.

"Nothing," she breathed, sliding to her knees. She drew my cock out, cradling it in her hands, and licked me from balls to tip in a long swipe.

My knees buckled.

I braced both forearms against the wall over her head, willing myself not to come in two seconds flat. Light fingers traced my length, and I bit back a groan Travis would have heard through his pain-killer induced sleep.

Her tongue flicked at the head of my cock until I was impossibly hard. With an almost secretive knowledge, her lips parted to swallow me whole. Her tongue swirled around my length as though she was Frenching it, which was a different level of heaven and hell wrapped in a pretty little package clad only in skin-tight jeans, kneeling at my feet.

"God, girl." I managed. My fingers wrapped in her luxurious curls, and I rested my closed fist gently against her head.

Natalie mumbled something, her head bobbing up and down and her mouth full. I choked back a laugh and a comment on manners, but I couldn't have made a coherent sentence if I tried. My balls drew up tight, and I willed myself back from the edge, lifting her into my arms.

"Stop, sweetheart. I need to be able to take care of you, too."

Will you be here tomorrow?

Would this be the last time I saw her, felt her against my body? I was glad I couldn't see her eyes to read the lie I'd let myself believe. My chest clenched in a deep ache, and I pulled her closer, needing her body pressed tight to mine.

"Plenty of time." Natalie nipped my collarbone playfilly and ran her tongue across my chest. Her fingers wrapped around my cock to jack me until I was back on the edge I'd managed to back down from unharmed.

"Fuck," I muttered. "Girl, you can't go doing something like that to a man and expect him to last." I gripped her wrists in my hands, prying them away from my body and sucked in long, deep breaths. "Jeans. Off." Those two words took all my willpower and more cohesive thought that I could muster.

"Yes, sir," she bantered.

That same playful note slamming me back to the brink of orgasm. Natalie wiggled her ass at me, and it took all I had not to smack it as hard as I could. But there was a reason I'd never made a habit of staying in the big house, never slept in the upstairs bedrooms.

I circled my arm around her waist, pulling her back tight against my chest. Her chest heaved as I ran one hand between her breasts, over her taut stomach to work the zip on her jeans. Then I slid my hand inside the lace panties beneath, over her soft folds. My fingers parted the swollen skin there, stroking along her drenched pussy but not entering her.

Not yet.

Natalie moaned softly, her head tilted back against my shoulder.

I brushed my mouth over hers and flicked my tongue over her ear lobe. My fingers played with her, stroking up and down, moving them in a waving motion that thrummed her sensitive skin.

"Jeans. Off. Now."

"What?" She blinked up at me, her hands already on her hips. I teased her again, merciless, and she let out a choked sob. "I can't—"

"Yes, you can." I pressed kisses to her mouth, running my tongue along her bottom lip, and sucked it into my mouth. My fingers never ceased, playing in the slick arousal that coated my hand.

She moaned and wriggled, which only added to her predicament. The moment her movement drew her away from my touch, the faster she pressed back to me. When her legs were caught, tangled in the denim, she bent forward, and I added a second hand to the mix, tugging at her budded nipples.

Her body trembled head to toe. She bore down on my fingers, though I refused to give her what she wanted. Finally freed from her jeans, she straightened, gripping my arm tight. Her hips bucked between us in a rhythm of her own, seeking friction.

"Jude, please," she whimpered.

I kissed her again, smiling against her mouth as I slipped my fingers inside her in a long thrust to the second knuckle. Curling them forward against the roughened skin inside her, I kept up that same playing motion until she clamped down on my hand in a series of tight flutters that matched her soft moans.

Her body arched back, taut as a bow string.

I slammed my mouth over hers, swallowing the remnants of her pleasure until she panted against my lips, soft and pliable in my arms.

"That's it, sweetheart. Good girl," I murmured.

I drew a condom out of my pocket. My face flamed in the darkness and I was glad she couldn't witness my discomfort. I kicked my own jeans off, and slid my arms beneath her legs to clasp her slight form to my chest.

Natalie tilted her head back, staring up at me. Her breath came in soft pants as I pulled the bedcovers down and laid her on the mattress.

"Help me out?" I passed her the little packet and knelt between her thighs.

The sweet scent of her pleasure filled my head until it spun. I slid her legs apart, encountering no resistance, and dipped to lick straight along her center, ending at her clit. The tight bundle of nerves hard stood against my tongue. I sucked gently, not enough to make her come again, just enough to placate her from the waves that still wracked her body in tiny aftershocks.

Her fingers tangled in my hair, and as her hips began to buck, she tugged me up. "Fill me, Jude. I need you deep."

I took the condom she offered, sliding the rubber over my aching cock. Her body heat emanated against my skin. I leaned over her, an arm braced on each side of her head, and dipped to catch her mouth, sliding my tongue between her lips as I entered her tight, hot body.

Natalie squeaked into my mouth, coming undone at the dual touch. The shudders that teased her in tiny waves hit her full on. She wrapped her legs around my hips, pushing me deeper.

"I thought we said slow," I murmured, giving the semblance of control that failed by the moment. My hips jerked, and I withdrew at the speed I had promised her, sliding in deep and just as slow.

"I can't—" she gasped, arching to meet my thrust.

"Yes you can," I coaxed, knowing she might hate me for a moment as I drew her pleasure away and plunged her back into it.

Nat's thighs trembled, and her tight little pussy clenched around me.

My hand found her hip. I dug my fingers into the soft, sensitive spot there, increasing our tempo until she bucked, clamping down and impossibly tight. All sensation ran from my balls drawn up into me to the tip of my cock and I came, my head buried into the slope of her shoulder. Her body shuddered around me. She clung to me, fighting her own pleasure, and finally succumbing to it in a series of sobs and moans.

I sank into her curves. My hips fit to hers in a perfect mold, a jigsaw piece pressed seamlessly together.

Her fingers tugged at my hair, and I pressed my mouth to hers. "My God, you're beautiful," I rasped.

She smiled against my lips. I pressed back, withdrawing in a long, slow movement. She shifted with me in a little inhale. I tied the condom off, disposing of it in the small bin behind the door and climbed back into Natalie's bed. The blankets fell around us both. She shifted to one side, her hands always touching me as though she couldn't bear to let go.

Understanding flooded me, and I drew her to me tight. "Spoon, or you want to sleep on my chest?" I brushed damp curls from her cheeks.

"Chest, please," she mumbled in a sleep laden voice.

"Done, gorgeous girl." I drew her head back for a slow kiss, rolling us so she sprawled across my chest.

The world blacked out, and I was asleep in an instant.

CHAPTER 9

Sunlight glared through my cracked eyelids as I dared to open them. The first thing to cross my mind was that it was well past dawn, a first for me in too many years to count. The second thing was that someone had been hammering on the door for a while. I rolled and nearly fell off the edge of the bed.

The other direction held a very warm and cuddly someone. I blinked and took in the walls of the spare room with little understanding, until the hammering started again.

"Jude. Get out here," Travis roared from the other side.

I blinked once more. My hand strayed across Natalie's naked back, tangling in loose locks that tumbled everywhere. A rueful smile curved my mouth. I climbed over her lithe form and yanked on last night's jeans.

The door flew back in my hand when I unlatched it. Trav stood on the other side, his fist halfway through a pounding knock.

"Get out here. We have a problem." Trav backed up a step on his crutches, his face a twisted grimace I was certain only added to his shitty mood.

"Good morning to you, too."

Travis shook his head. "It's not. We have dead deer. And it's her fault." He pointed behind me.

I swiveled on my heel to stare at Natalie, who must have dressed at record speed.

Her shirt was slightly rumpled, and her hair was thrown up in a messy ponytail, but otherwise she looked as she had during the day. Every trace of sleep had been erased from her face, and there was a hardness to her jawline that hadn't been there before.

I missed the soft lines of her naked curves, and my cock stirred in an instant. I swiped a hand over my face and resisted slapping myself in a wake up call.

"Come again?" I winced and waited for the rejoinder, but silence hung in the hall between the three of us, tense and still.

"Dead. Deer." Trav pointed down the stairs. "Eve will set you straight. You," he pointed behind me, "I need to speak with you about cross contamination."

"We can talk downstairs."

"There isn't a risk."

Natalie and my words collided.

She folded her arms over her chest and glared at Travis. "And here I was going to offer you a hand to get down, but I don't think that ego of yours will let me take its weight."

"Don't you get smart, little girl. You may have just ruined the finest herd in northern Montana."

Natalie clucked her tongue. "Those elk are as healthy as any animal at a sale yard. Let me go down and see what's happened."

"I'm not letting you anywhere near my stock. This reeks of sabotage."

I frowned. "That's pushing it. If anything, it's my fault. You sent me out to get something, and I chose poorly."

"I'll speak to you later about this." Trav dismissed me.

I raised my eyebrows, debating whether it was okay to punch my best friend when he was still on crutches.

Natalie raised a hand. "I have no idea what you're talking about, but before you smear the reputation I've worked so hard to build, I'd like to see what's happened."

"Go right ahead." Travis all but sneered as he waved her away. He leaned his crutches against the wall, and braced his back to it for balance and support.

It was more than I could give him at that moment.

Natalie's eyes narrowed as she stared up at him. Her gaze flicked to mine, and I read uncertainty in their azure depths. Then she was halfway down the stairs, Trav's crutches clutched under one arm, before I could say a thing.

"That was uncalled for," I said in a low voice, though I knew it would carry. "You might have woken up an asshole, but it's a choice to stay that way."

"You haven't seen what I have." Travis motioned to the stairs. "I'll show you."

I folded my arms and didn't move. "Some manners would go a long way."

"What the hell are you on about?" Travis stared. "Do I have to worry you're part of this, too?"

"Part of what, exactly? You accuse a woman who was scared to come back here in the event you threw her out, or didn't like the choice I'd made on your damn behalf, and had to resell the thing all over again."

"Scared? More like guilty. Come on." He gestured impatiently.

I held my ground. "Please."

Travis rolled his eyes and put on his best falsetto. "Please, Jude, would you fucking help me to get down the stairs to see the calamity your new girlfriend brought to Red Hart." He batted his eyelashes, glaring at me.

If his tone hadn't been laced with animosity, I might have laughed. "If I tell you to get your own way down, what are you going to do? Be fucking pleasant. It will get you further," I snarled at him. It took some working around but I managed to get my shoulder into its familiar position under his.

I bore his weight the entire way in strained silence, though I suspected Natalie was right. His ego was the heaviest part. To be fair, Travis had struggled with mobility, lost two parents, and had two semi-successful operations in the last four months. It was enough to drive any man crazy. We hit the ground floor, and I sucked in a deep breath.

"Why do you think someone is sabotaging Red Hart?" It was the only thing of everything he had said that stuck in my head.

Travis could have demanded to see papers from Natalie, to prove she ran a fair business, and registered her herds. He could have asked her about any disease or parasite, but he'd jumped straight to a far-fetched conclusion.

I needed to know where in the hell his ideas were coming from.

"Pierce MacQuid turned up on our doorstep early this morning, escorted by his elderly father."

"Black Hill Boy." I smiled at Archer's nickname for the heir of our largest neighbor. "What did he want?"

"His father is sick, and he hoped Eve would help him. Then he asked her out."

I froze, my mind honing in on that one piece of information and discarding the other. "He what?" Pierce had always been an odd kid, the sort who tried to fit in and failed magnificently. His lanky frame was unsuited to yard work, and he would have fit better in a city maybe, working office politics. Hard work was for honest men, even if they were a pack of assholes. It seemed to be my theme of the day, and I hadn't had coffee yet.

Maybe there was sense to that. I made a promise to myself to make one for Trav before he got any worse.

"Yeah. He pushed a bit, but eventually she told him she was involved with someone."

I winced. "Not hard to work out who."

Travis' mouth twitched, and I could have sworn he was about to smile. "Yeah. He wasn't none too happy about it. Bill laughed at her. It's not okay to drop an old man, but by God I wanted to. Fuck him. She spotted the deer in the yard and came running back inside. They were a bit mangy looking first up apparently, then they dropped. Two of them. I saw it from my bedroom window," he added defensively. He crossed one arm over his chest, clinging to the crutches Natalie had left at the bottom of the stairs.

"Okay, so, let's go and see them. Seeing Pierce made you think he was up to something?"

"Apart from creeping on my sister?" Travis' mouth twisted away from the smile that had been growing there. "Yeah."

154

"All right. Come on." I gripped his shoulder hard and propelled us both out of the door, kneeling to fit his boots while he balanced in the doorway. "You notice Eve is tired?"

Trav huffed a laugh. "We all are."

"I know that."

But she looks sick.

A knot tangled in the pit of my stomach and started to grow.

Cool air with a warm wind behind it brushed my cheeks. I grabbed my jacket in one hand, hat in the other and steadied Trav down the few veranda steps to get him onto solid ground. Once I was sure he'd be all right to make his own way across the yard, I headed for the small knot of people on the other side.

Halfway there, I turned back. "Did you call Rachel?"

Travis nodded, his teeth bared in a pained grimace.

I gave him a wave and headed for a shirt I recognised, throwing my jacket over my shoulders. "Gage. Can I get through?"

Dark gray eyes so usually filled with humor turned on me. "Yeah, sure."

Natalie and Eve knelt around a deer that twisted between them. Natalie had one knee on its hind quarters and ran her hands over the doe's ribs.

"So not dead, then." I squatted next to them, and rested one hand on Eve's back. "I heard about Pierce. Are you okay?"

She shrugged my hand away. "Fine. But what's happening here?" Her brow furrowed.

"I don't know. Trav said he was worried about mange, but she looks fine to me." The doe's reddish brown coat glimmered with the thick sheen of a healthy animal beneath the early morning sun. "And he freaked out that Natalie sabotaged the herd." I barked a laugh that rasped in my throat.

"So she said." Eve traced over the deer's hind quarters with a gentle finger.

"And?" I pushed, already testy after my confrontation with Travis. "Your twin was in fine form this morning."

"He's upset you got laid and he can't get anywhere with Rachel. Can we turn her over?"

"Ah, move back." I motioned to Natalie. "I've got this."

Together, Eve and I manhandled the poor thing, though its kicking grew weaker until it lay placid without us holding it. "What just happened?" The deer's eye fluttered closed. Had the damn thing died on us?

"I don't know." Eve ran a hand over the doe's mouth, tugging it back to study her gums.

I pressed a hand to her ribs, but breath still flowed through her still body. Relief sluiced through me, though the thought Travis had planted not ten minutes ago took root. Guilt swamped me, and I snuck a glance sideways at Eve, who gave no indication of what passed through her mind.

Dark circles shadowed her stunning face, leaving her angular and drawn.

"Okay, we have to talk about a few things." I brought my hand away from the deer's hindquarters and stopped. Blood stretched my fingers in a fine line. "What the—" I traced back to where I had touched her leg. A small red dot announced the site of the puncture, but there was only one I could see. "Not a snake bite."

Eve leaned closer. "No. Jude, can you collect a tiny sample, please? I want Rachel to test it."

A silver truck pulled up into the yard behind us as she spoke, and another dark-haired woman got out, though Rachel's hair was cut a lot shorter than either Natalie or Eve's.

"Yeah, sure." I patted my pockets in an old habit and rose. My muscles ached. "I'll be right back."

Natalie glanced up at me and rose as well, though she had a whole lot more grace than me. "I'd like to check the elk. Can someone show me where they went?"

"Kyle," I shouted to a young cowboy standing at the back of the knot of men still huddled together, all whispering like a cluck of

158

damn hens. "Take Natalie up to the elk. Johnny will show you where we put them."

I checked around a few heads, all boys I knew from the bunk house. Johnny waved at me from the edge of the crowd, loitering, and gave me a confirming nod. Relieved that at least one of the girls was in good hands, I headed for the barn and the locker where we stored all the ranch's livestock supplements and a small stock of medical equipment for the herd. I grabbed swabs and a baggie and headed back out to Eve.

Travis leaned against the fence, his lips pulled tight. His gaze tracked Rachel as she moved around the deer. He gripped the railing like he wanted to strangle it.

I couldn't work out whether it was because of the pain or because the deer was alive. The traitorous thought stuck with me, but I banished it from wherever it had originated. I walked straight through the crowd clustered to one side of the proceedings with a cough. The boys shifted, letting me through. The deer didn't look any better than it had a few minutes ago, though Rachel staunched the blood flow with a gauze pad. I offered her the swabs and baggie, but it was Eve who took them.

"Thanks." She waited until Rachel was finished, holding them out in silence.

The girls moved seamlessly in the concerto of people who had worked together for many years.

"Maybe it fell on a stick or a thorn got it?" Eve murmured. She looked to Rachel for confirmation.

The vet shook her head. "I don't think so, unless it was a very specific thorn, because..." She swung around, revealing a smaller doe I hadn't noticed that huddled behind a stationary quad bike. "Because this little girl has the same mark."

I frowned. "An animal attack, maybe? Snake bite?"

The doe stirred, twitching. Rachel did a few more cheeks, and helped the creature get to its feet, albeit wobbly.

"She'll be okay. Possible snake bite, but it's high, and there's only one mark on each animal. I'll test the blood, see what comes up. We might have to wait a bit for results if I have to send anything away. Are there any more?"

Eve shook her head. "Not deer. I think there's another wounded animal who needs you." She smiled, brushing her hair back from her face. The lines there were drawn tighter than ever, and I realized with a start just how much she resembled Travis' suffering.

The difference was that Eve did hers in silence, while Trav made a production out of it. I knew where my loyalties lay, and I was far more inclined to take Eve's side...especially when my best friend seemed hell bent on blaming Natalie for something that had nothing to do with her.

Eve pushed up to her feet in what should have been a fluid movement, but wasn't. She stayed bent at the waist for half a minute, a hand pressed to her lower back.

I shooed the crowd away, throwing jobs for the day to each face as they turned my way, anything to give the twins a bit of space.

Rachel packed up her things and spared Eve a small glance, but her attention was fixed on Travis. Eve's twin's eyes narrowed, and he grabbed his crutches, making his way back to the house at a painfully slow gait.

"He's in a terrible mood," Eve said to the deer. "But I'm sure he'll be better soon."

"Will you?" The words tumbled from my open mouth. I slammed it shut with an audible clack, cursing silently in my head.

Eve's worn gaze lighted to meet mine. I held my ground, prepared to weather whatever beating she needed to throw my way. She sent me the same, tired smile and patted the doe's rump on its unmarred side, sending it skittering across the field, though not quite at its usual speed.

"Things take time, Jude. I'm glad you're back." She walked away from me at the pace of an older woman.

I stared.

Eve had never been or looked old. Nothing was a problem for her, and she had energy to spare, but this...it was the world weary step of an exhausted person. Of someone who had given up.

Bile rose in my throat, and I swallowed it back with effort. The other doe took a few tentative steps and followed in its predecessor's path, leaving me alone in the yard. I leaned over the railing, turning my hat in my hands.

A gust of wind showered me in grit and grass, the dying edge of autumn in its icy tendrils, though we were halfway through spring. I fought back a shiver and jammed my hat on my head. If I couldn't make a difference with the twins, maybe I could with Nat. Braving their wrath—Travis' at least—I headed back into the house to grab my phone.

CHAPTER 10

I stared at the empty pregnancy kit in my hand. A simple trip for a civilized leak had turned into something so much bigger. My mind was still playing catch up, but there was only one person in the house it could belong to—well, unless that person wasn't in the house at all. I'd forgotten that both Travis and Eve shared the upstairs bathroom, never having used it in my life, preferring to stay downstairs, and with the evidence of the past twelve hours, I wish I'd stayed down there.

Which begged the question...who? Rachel? I couldn't imagine Travis getting laid in his current state, let alone having the swimmers to get anyone pregnant. Unfortunately being a grumpy asshole had nothing to do with the ability to produce a child.

My mind flocked back to Eve, how she'd looked, and I cursed. I threw the box on the bathroom counter and headed back to the spare room, fumbling about the bed for my phone. It fell out from beneath the pillow, and I was halfway through a message to Archer before I threw it back on the bed.

Had Eve told him? It wasn't my place to break news like that to a man, and seeing as he was at the opposite end of the country working a case that couldn't release him, it was cruel to boot.

There was still the doubt that Rachel could be the owner of the kit, and she and Travis had spent more time together than ever. Not that they were closer, exactly, more that Rachel tried to be closer to him, and Travis pushed her away at every available moment. His attitude was wearing thin.

Apparently, a few days away from Red Hart had given me a fresh perspective on the people who lived and worked beside me on a day-to-day basis.

I suppressed the urge to return to the bathroom and filter through the bin for the results the kit had yielded, sickened at the thought of prying into someone else's life. But this was my Eve, and her health and mental state mattered to me. To have to go it alone because her man couldn't be with her for something that would be precious to both of them...I swore violently under my breath. Archer would want to be with her, would move mountains to be beside her. Which meant either I was wrong, or she hadn't told him.

I pocketed my phone, grinding my teeth, and headed back down stairs.

Eve leaned against the long, heavy wooden counter, a coffee mug between her hands, staring into space.

I stalked toward her and stopped a few feet away. "Why haven't you told him?"

Eve turned to me in slow motion, recognition flaring in her gaze for a single instant. It faded faster than it had come on, and she shook her head.

"That's got nothing to do with you."

I raised both eyebrows and closed the space between us. "Nothing to do with me? I see this." I cupped her cheek and grazed my thumb over the shadows beneath her eyes, the sallow skin that usually bottled her formidable energy behind it. "And I don't get to care?"

"You've never noticed before." Eve shrugged. She lifted her mug to her lips, touching them but not drinking from it.

That stung. It really fucking stung, and not only because I knew she was right.

"Don't you hide from me," I growled, letting my anger out in a sliding scale that threatened eruption. "I'm sorry I didn't see it before, but you're not well, Eve. Have you been to a doctor? Why haven't you said something?"

"There's nothing to be said."

I scoffed, disregarding the warning that flared in her hazelwood eyes. "I think the man who gave everything for you would like to know. How about your brother? Shouldn't he know—"

"Shhhh." Eve's eyes flashed again, more frantic this time, and she yanked away from my touch.

I lowered the hand I hadn't realized was still raised in my righteous anger, anger that fizzled and died at the panic I read in her face. "Eve?"

Her eyes welled. "Trav isn't going to be an uncle. Not now, maybe not ever. Not after what—" She choked on the tears that cascaded down her face, fumbling behind her to place her mug blindly on the counter. "I can conceive, but I can't c—carry."

A lump rose in my throat. "Oh, hell." I wound my arms around her tight, pulling her into my chest. "Is this after what that asshole did to you?"

She nodded into my chest, leaving a damp spot in her wake, but I didn't care. I rocked her gently in my arms, weathering the shuddering sobs that poured from her. Had she told anyone else at all? Not likely, by the way emotion flooded from her in an endless deluge. She'd held it all in, and I'd attacked her at the first chance.

Nice work, Jude.

"I'm sorry, sweetie. I'm so sorry." I kissed the top of her head, forming a barrier with my body between her and the rest of the world. How much weight had she lost? "I'm sorry I didn't notice, Evie. It's— hell. There's no justification."

"It's okay," she mumbled against my chest. Her body was so frail. "But, please, Jude. You can't tell anyone. They'll make a huge fuss, and I'll have to go to d—doctors and be examined like I'm an experiment to see what works and I can't face it!" Her voice ended on a high note, hysteria blossoming in her gaze.

"I promise I won't tell anyone, and I promise I won't let anyone take you anywhere." I cradled her tear stained cheeks, lifting her face to mine. "I promise. Is it possible this happened because of grief? Of your mom?" I held my breath.

Yet another thing that wasn't spoken about between the twins, or anywhere at Red Hart. The morning I'd walked into the barn and found a pool of blood surrounding Betty's body, her late husband's razor blade in her torn grip.

Two of the boys had helped me clean up after the formalities were observed, and that was that. A somber melancholy had fallen over Red Hart, and the pall only just lifted in the last month.

Silence filled the house. I had no idea where Travis and Rachel had gotten to, but I was glad to have Eve to myself for the time being. Trying to process the right course of action in the presence of others wasn't a palatable move.

I pressed my lips together, thought better of the idea rolling around in my head, and said it anyway. "You need to tell him."

Eve shook her head. "No."

"Please, Eve. He deserves to know."

"No."

"He would want to know, and he could help you—"

"Help me what? Feel like a failure? I can't even be a mother, I'm that bad at it. Neglect? Grief? Because my body can't?" She shook her head. Deep garnet waves shimmered in a cascade of their own over her too-slim shoulders.

"He could support you and give you love."

"No." She clung to the word with every inch of her old determination, and that stubbornness gave me hope.

I smiled and brushed my thumb over her cheek. "Don't you dare give in."

"No chance." She hiccuped a laugh.

I rested my forehead against hers as the faint echo filled in the empty house. The sound dropped away to leave us in a still and pensive silence, a void, except for the door that clicked shut at my back.

Eve frowned at me and peered around my shoulder. "Oh no."

"Fuck. It's Natalie, isn't it?"

Eve tried to detangle herself from my arms. "Um. Yeah. Well, it was—"

"Fuck." I held on tight.

"Language," she reprimanded me. "Go."

I covered my laugh with a cough when she sent me a stern glance. "Are you sure? You're not going to, you know..." I let the thought dangle.

"Hurt myself?" she raised an eyebrow. "No, Jude. If I was going to do that, it would have happened already."

"That's not reassuring."

"I'm just tired."

"Then rest, sweetie. Let me hold up my end of the bargain."

"What bargain is that?" Her brow dipped.

I smoothed it with my thumb. "The one where you and Trav retire, and I'll be the muck around farm boy."

"I think Kyle might have a few years on you in that department. You're more the crabby old man."

"Gee, thanks."

"Go." She pushed both hands to my chest and shoved.

"Are you sure you're all right?"

173

"Go, Jude." Eve rolled her eyes. Pink stained her cheeks, giving her the look of her old self as the corners of her mouth turned up.

Finally, I took heed from the woman of the house, and left.

I pushed the doors to the ranch house open and jumped the few steps. My boots hit the ground in a puff of dust that grew as I jogged across the yard to where Natalie's truck stood. Her back was presented to me, her arms waving as she gave Johnny a rapid fire set of instructions.

Light blue eyes met mine over her shoulder and the abject fear in them gave me pause. Of me? I watched Johnny scurry around the back of the truck with narrowed eyes. No. More likely, he was afraid of Natalie's temper, or what we would become together.

Natalie followed her cowboy's line of sight over her shoulder and faced me square on.

I might have expected hands on her hips, or maybe a defiant stance of some sort, but not the glittering eyes and the tears that cascaded down her cheeks at the sight of me.

"Natalie." I jogged the last few paces and slowed to a trot, coming to a standstill before her. "What are you doing?"

"What does it look like I'm doing?" Even through her tears, her glance was incredulous. "I'm packing up. After what I've seen and what I've been through today I'm. Going. Home." She punctuated every word with a poke to my chest, and for a moment, her tears stopped.

I stepped into her space, curving my palms to fit firm around her waist. "Stay."

"Are you being serious?" She pushed my hands away. "Jude. Not only am I not welcome here and my business could take a massive freaking down curve because of the man in there who will not listen to reason, but I also can't stay around you."

I clenched my teeth. "Because of what you think you saw."

"Because of what I know I saw," she countered.

175

Her hair swung wildly across her shoulders. My fingers itched to touch her, the need to bring her close too much.

"It's not what you think." The thought of Eve in my bed was laughable. The thought of grimy old me in hers was even worse. "I can't go there, Nat."

"No? Then tell me what it's about."

I clenched my teeth. "I can't."

"Gee, funny, that."

My promise to Eve suddenly semmed like a real fucking bad idea. "Seriously, I can't, but please—"

"Please stay around so you can fuck me while I screw around with my other non-girlfriend behind your back? No thanks." Natalie gestured Johnny inside the passenger door of the truck and slammed the door behind him. "Bye, Jude. I wish—" She swallowed and disappeared in a flurry of chestnut curls and ocean blue eyes.

The image burned instantly into my memory and would haunt me for the next week, month...year.

My mouth was still open to protest when she drove around in a large circle in the yard and disappeared down the drive.

"That went well." Travis's deep voice surrounded me, and I resisted the urge to punch him.

"How the fuck did you creep up on me, you damn invalid?" I pushed out air between clenched teeth.

"Not hard when you've got your head up your ass."

"And you can talk."

"Probably not." Trav leaned on his crutches, his arms folded over them. "You going to be all right?"

No, because you've pushed away the only woman I've been close to in years.

Though half of it was my fault, at the least. Natalie must have seen me with Eve, and then the way I'd handled the situation...poor didn't come close to covering it.

My jaw ached, and I pried my teeth apart long enough to answer him. "Did you keep the stock?"

"Yep."

"Did you pay her for them?"

"Am I that much of an asshole?"

"Right now? Yes." I slammed my boot into the hard-packed ground. Dust bunnies rose in tiny explosions. "I need to get some work done, even if you don't." Clouds puffed around my boots as I spun on my heel and started for my own truck, head down.

Travis' hand caught my shoulder as I turned, and he grunted at the jerky movement. "Don't be a dick just because you were caught out flirting with my sister." There was an undercurrent in his voice, a dark warning I was too blind or too intentionally stpuid to appreciate.

I answered him without turning back. "That's not what this is about."

"Then what is it about?" Trav's voice held a pleading note this time.

178

That he was Eve's twin hit me fully. Of course he'd seen her drawn face, her lackluster appearance. They'd just lost a mother to grief and depression. Now, he worried he would lose her, too.

What had been a thriving family four months ago was whittled down to two broken siblings, aged beyond their years in a few short months. Still, I'd promised her, and with everything else fucked up in all our lives right now, I wasn't going to break that.

"It's not my secret to tell."

CHAPTER II

The boys who bunked in with me away from the big house got used to a grueling routine in the weeks that followed. Hard work, the sort that started well before dawn and ran until I couldn't see my hands in front of my face, was the only way I knew to stave off the loneliness and heartbreak. It had worked a treat for the last fifteen years, and I saw no reason to stop now.

Dealing with the loss of Natalie was like suffering a type of grief, albeit a different sort to the ones both Trav and Eve did.

A broken bunch of fools still carrying on.

"The field's done, boss." Gage tipped his hat up to slog water from an old plastic bottle. The scar that stripped him from eyebrow to jawline moved with him, stretching his skin in an uncorrelated tightness.

Like most of the loners who arrived for a season or two of work before they departed to lose themselves in a different part of the country, Gage brought a single small duffle bag containing only the shirt on his back and two spare pairs of worn jeans, an ancient leather bible and a silver-lined turquoise hammered cuff.

I'd given him-and every man who worked under me-hell while I fought the heady drive to walk away from Travis and his knowing gaze, get in my truck and spend the five hours on the black top working out what I'd do with Natalie when I saw her again.

But duty came first, and with no reprieve in sight, I went hell for leather in my work and brought everyone else along with me.

Not one of them folded, and Gage led the charge. For that he got my respect, my ear and a whole lot of more work to do.

When I asked him about the two personal items, he'd given me an easy shrug. "One is from family, and one is for family. I just don't know who I'm giving it to yet."

He hadn't offered more information, and I hadn't asked.

Dusk blanketed the landscape behind him in a hazy purple. The boys milled around, some pulling off battered leather working gloves to replace them with the warmer variety they preferred while others collected tools, still padding around the field in search of the next job.

Creating new fence lines to segregate the two herds had been a mammoth task, but we had managed with a small adjoining section to go. At the rate we were working, it would be tipped over by the end of the week.

Guilt twinged at me that I'd taken them away from what should have been a usual routine of showering before they hit the big house for dinner, but if we waited any longer, Eve would be in bed, and Travis would be pissed.

I zipped my vest and called to down tools. "All right. Get back to the house, fill yourselves up. We'll start here, work to the corner, then this section is done. Gage, you're lead tomorrow."

Gage nodded, shooting me a sideways look as he spoke quietly to the men assembling around him.

"Good. We can get up at dawn, not work in the moonlight," someone—I couldn't see who—muttered.

I opened the door of my truck and flicked on the lights—anything to dispel the impatience that rose in me. Part of me wanted to throw out a comeback, but this was Gage's job. In the end, I didn't need to say anything.

"Nah, for that, you can meet me out here for a morning jog, princess." Gage grinned, his silhouette half illuminated in the glow the headlights provided. "And if you bitch about it, we're on clean up duty tonight." Someone groaned in the background. Gage made a pistol out of his forefinger and thumb, cocking it at the unfortunate soul. "That's us."

Laughter ran around the small group as they worked their way back to the trucks parked off to one side and loaded up their tools and equipment. A lot of the bigger supplies were left out, but I refused to leave perfectly good tools out overnight. The military side of Gage appealed to my sense of work ethic.

He waited 'til the last truck joined the convoy heading back to the big house before he climbed into my truck and threw on the heat. Despite coming into late spring, the nights were still cold enough.

"Where are you going tomorrow?"

"Who said I was going anywhere?"

"I didn't take you for a mankini guy, but hey, if you want to sunbake and take a day off, be my guest." He fell silent, waiting for a response that was never coming. "Still thinking about her?"

"Fuck off."

Gage's laughter filled the cab of my truck as I followed everyone else back to the house.

The ex-soldier was as good as his word and had everyone up, fed, and active by half four. Eve hadn't come down, breaking her usual habit, so I fed the troops in her absence, forcing myself to concentrate on the food prep rather than worry about her. Gage gave me a jaunty wave as he pushed the last stragglers out the door, filled with bacon, eggs, and fresh rye bread I'd thrown on the night before.

I filled three tall travel mugs with steaming coffee, each branded with RHR in the heart and antlers logo.

Travis stirred on the sofa as I placed one by his head. He'd maintained his sour outlook at life in general, and I'd kept my distance.

But the truth was that I missed my best friend, missed the banter, missed working shoulder to shoulder with him. Gage was a great worker, and I actually liked the man, but he had the look in his eyes of a man who had already overstayed in one location. If we got this job finished and still had him on board, I'd be surprised.

The house sat quiet in the pre-dawn light. Travis snored softly on the sofa, falling back into a deep sleep now the boys had left for the day. I placed Eve's cup in the middle of the kitchen counter so she couldn't possibly miss it. The things were insulated as hell, and even if she didn't get up until well after the sun rose, it would still be warm enough to drink.

I took a long sip of scalding coffee, grabbed my jacket from the hook outside the door, jammed my boots and hat on, and headed for my truck. It would be a hell of a convoluted drive to get up to Natalie's place, but it would be worth it.

Weeks on and I hadn't been able to forget her. Maybe it was because I hadn't had a casual relationship in a while, or maybe it was the deep-seated craving that drove a need to believe it had been something more.

Natalie's expression, utterly broken and betrayed, yet still fired up, haunted me daily until the most I could do about it was to jerk off to the memory of her in the shower, and tumble into my empty bed exhausted, wishing I could touch her.

I pulled out of Red Hart's entrance and turned left, heading deeper into the mountains. A small border security post lay a few hours along the drive, which sure beat driving out hundreds of miles in the path Natalie had said she used. But the open road and a half day's drive appealed to me at a deeper level. Even the ranch house had gotten too noisy for me—I needed the time away. And getting off the land, for a rare once, actually felt good.

Brantley Gilbert sang about holding his last breath. I cranked the song up, if for no other reason than to numb my brain and let someone else's voice fill it.

I flashed my passport at the office and was through the gate in record time. The sun flared in my eyes, the road heavily wooded as I moved deeper into the country and took a minor unpaved road toward Granite Falls.

The call I needed to make weighed on me, and naturally, I procrastinated about it until I entered the thick treeline and lost all reception.

The forest loomed over me, still and silent as I tore through it. My mind flitted back to Natalie—meeting her in the saleyards, flirting with her at the bar, her body pressed to mine as we danced. The night we spent together, discovering each other in the pitch black of her truck.

Rather than bring on a raging dose or arousal, my heart ached for the contours of her body molded to mine. A few days together and I'd fallen head over boots for a woman I barely knew but wanted all the same.

A girl who, I'd come to realize, was likely as wealthy as the twins, which made her a millionaire in her own right, and I was just a poor farm boy, a runaway who had found a home but still had nothing of my own to offer her.

The first driveway flashed by, bringing me out of my reverie. I slowed, counting the miles until a small, unadorned gate marked Crossman had me pulling up. The gate was open, and I debated for a long moment, but I'd come too far to chicken out now.

I turned down the well-graded drive at walking pace, my gaze flitting from side to side as I took in the shadows of animals beginning larger tree trunks. Where Red Hart was open fields and fresh air for the most part, until the mountain foothills joined with a series of rocky outcrops, Granite Falls was completely treed in, at least as far as I could see. If she had grassy fields on the other side of the woods, I couldn't see it.

A flash drew my attention. I pulled around a bend with care and stopped my truck in the middle of the open drive. A handsome redwood house sat in the center of a small clearing, though it had been designed to include the surrounding trees. Some formed pillars at corners of the veranda, others created copses clustered at each side to form a crescent circle behind the house, framing it.

The mountain rose somewhere above the house, but it was shrouded in white clouds, which blotted out everything above the treeline.

I closed my mouth and steered the truck off to one side of the stunning ranch house, though my attention drifted to the matching black and white rigs, sparkling together. I parked my much filthier truck beside them, much resembling the destitute cousin. Something about that black truck bothered me. I stared at it, waiting for the penny to drop, but the bank was empty after the long drive and the need to see Natalie again.

My boots hit the damp ground covered in a soft bed of pine needles. Air clouded around my mouth as I exhaled, and I appreciated the mountain's cold, late spring kiss. Natalie's home had some serious elevation on Red Hart.

I strode the short distance to the house, my hand raised to knock on the large glass doors set in a heavy redwood frame, but I didn't need to; the door already stood open. My fist raised to knock I paused, staring intently into the depths of the hall.

Voices filtered back at me, but I ignored those, making out a familiar shape, and not one I expected to see. A dark head swung my way, and Pierce made a show of parting his open shirt. His gaze weighed on me every passing second, until I slammed one boot into the floorboards, unable to contain my frustration any longer.

CHAPTER 12

Pierce flashed me a shit eating grin and began to button his shirt, his eyes trained deeper into the dark interior of Natalie's house.

I took one step into the dark and hallway and saw a second shadowy figure. Natalie's fingers grazed along with her jaw as she spotted me and hers dropped, along with her hand, though I felt her phantom touch on my own bristled skin.

"Thanks, Natalie." Pierce dipped his head to brush his lips over her cheek.

My stomach roiled. Pierce passed me before I could make myself move, still fiddling with the buttons on his shirt. A long scar, pink and puckered, decorated his chest before he completed buttoning his pearl-lined shirt. Dressed in his customary black he looked as sleek and oily as he usually did, a ward to every person I knew who came into contact with him...with the possible exception of Natalie and Eve, who obviously adored him. The churning in my throat brought bile bubbling to the back of my throat. I swallowed it back, willing myself not to punch Travis's neighbor on the spot.

He was in his truck before I made it back over the threshold, my own boots following in his wake without conscious thought. Bare feet padded the floorboards behind me.

"Jude, wait!"

"What for?" I jammed my key into the ignition and cranked it so hard the ignition screeched. I didn't care. All I needed was to get out of there, and yet I stood in Natalie's yard, inactive as a redwood, standing in a cloud of Pierce's dust.

This is the second time in a few weeks that he's bested me.

Natalie's small hand pressed to my back in a gentle touch my body more than recognized. I didn't turn back to her or acknowledge her, but neither did she retreat.

The classic stand off.

Breath sucked into my lungs, not as controlled as I would have liked, but icier, not the fresh air I remembered savoring around her. "Please stay."

It was the only catch in our impasse. Which of us would break first? My stubborn streak flared, and hers rose to match it.

"Why should I?"

"Because I've missed you."

I snorted at the meaningless words. My head was still awhirl at the thought that she could accuse me of betrayal when she was doing essentially the same thing. Belatedly, perhaps, but my brain wasn't interested in arguing semantics.

The quiver at the end of her words that she tried to hide in a hard tone gave me pause. I stopped back, taking her in fully for the first time in weeks. The seductive image that met my gaze with sapphire and ice stole my breath, my heart and likely a good slab of my soul along with it.

She wore a stormy blue long sleeved V-neck tee that clung to every curve—and she had plenty of those—leaving the swell of her breast and nipples visible. Loose, auburn locks draped over her shoulders, framing the same heart-shaped face I'd fallen in love with on the first day I had met her.

The thought slammed into me with the force of a supersonic jet. I swallowed hard, not bothering to deny it, and shifted on my feet, aching against the need to adjust myself, and willed my body and brain to retain some semblance of control.

Forcing back the lump in my throat that refused to budge, I spoke around it, grating out the words as best I could. "Yeah, well, I've missed you too. But I didn't expect to see Red Hart's archenemy—I mean our fabulous neighbor—half-naked in your hallway, or you like this." I gestured at her with an open palm. My gaze locked onto her breasts, my fingers aching to touch her, to feel the weight of her luscious flesh beneath my hands, but this was about more than sex.

Okay, so I was lying to myself.

It mostly wasn't about sex.

The thought of working through each day without Natalie there...without anyone to talk it over with, pulled the proverbial rug out from me. A fresh, mountain scented one that had her unique mark branded to it.

Natalie shook her head. Curls danced around her face. "It's not like that, Jude. I didn't know he was coming any more than I knew you'd be here."

I snorted at that. Every smart assed comment that rolled around in my head was only guaranteed to get me in deeper trouble, so I refrained, but the sneer came through in my voice all the same. "I'm sorry I didn't announce myself."

Hell, I was sorry I'd made the drive at all. Natalie closed her fine-boned hand around mind, switching off the ignition. It wasn't a power move, as I could have stopped her or thrown her off; more that a small part of me wanted her to explain and welcome me back.

How pathetic have I become?

"We had a dispute over some stock that wandered from his place to mine." She tilted her head back, locking that azure gaze onto mine.

I read no defiance there, only a simmering warning. It was a pathetic attempt at a distraction. "Bullshit." I wasn't playing this game, or any other with her after the last weeks of hell. "You don't have the same herd. He runs cattle. You run elk." That Natalie ran her own cattle as well hit me too late, and the words were out.

Who was it that didn't want to argue semantics?

Some part of me wanted to check out how she had set up her herds and make sure that what I'd done a Red Hart to segregate our herds was correct. Not that it was necessary, but I wanted to make sure we got things right from the get go.

"It's not my livestock that wandered onto my lands though his fence line." She stared at me, her blue eyes wide and guileless. "It was yours."

A harsh breath sucked into my chest. I held it there, relished the pressure, anything as a distraction. Fucking Pierce again. And I'd let him walk away without that punch, which I was regretting fast. "Fantastic, so you provide the elk, and then you steal them back through our common neighbor."

"That's not fair." Natalie shot me a betrayed glance.

That one swings both ways, sweetheart.

She blinked, confusion crossing her face at whatever she chose to read in mine, and her gaze dropped to the ground.

I followed it to her bare feet, and part of my brain recognized just how frigid the air was in the shadow of the trees. The soft, damp earth underfoot held none of the residual warmth of the day that Red Hart got, unless I delved deep into the woods at the wrong time of the year. "You must be freezing."

The corner of her mouth quirked in a brief half-smile that died before I could savor it. "Come inside?"

I froze for the second time, caught in a tug-o-war between brain and heart. Though my brain screamed at me, I went with the obvious fall back option and extended my hand in invitation, or maybe it was acceptance.

Whose battle I sided on had muddled with the need to pull her into my arms and keep her there. The brain had clearly lost this round.

Fingers pressed to mine and closed around my roughened palm. Her grip was still soft, but she had plenty of her own scars. I liked that our callouses matched. What was it about this woman that wouldn't allow me to let her go?

Natalie led me back into the house. I paused to kick my boots off at the doorway, as though making my presence known. Territorial displays had never been my thing, but Natalie brought out a long dormant part of me I'd forgotten how to repress.

Inside the house, redwood continued to dominate, keeping in theme of what I'd grasped from my brief glimpse of the hallway. She and her late husband had built the house together, I recalled, and I could see her taste etched into the arched doorways and the blue edged rugs that softened our footfalls as we progressed through the house.

The hall opened to a wide living area that included a white countered kitchen off to one side. A walkway turned a corner to what I assumed was a pantry or another living area. What held my attention was the giant fireplace, and the thousands upon thousands of books that lined the walls in every conceivable space, stacked one atop the other in double rows.

Above the leather sofa hung a giant, triple-stacked antler chandelier. The usage wasn't usually to my taste, as it was frequently a hunter's trophy. However, with Natalie, I knew the likelihood was that she had collected the things and put them together herself from shed pairs wild males dropped each season.

I ran my fingers along the worn dust jacket tattered at the base, and pulled one from its spot. The top was a bit dusty, but the spine was frayed and soft where she must have rubbed her thumb as she read. I didn't recognize more than a fifth of the titles, but I was grateful to have some extra knowledge of her.

This woman who had captured my heart was still such an enigma to me, considering I'd spent nights aching for her in my arms.

"Natalie. What was he doing here?" I asked the same question as before, but laden it with a very different meaning and prayed that she understood what I was asking, unable to tack my real question onto the one I voiced.

Her lips parted, and I knew she heard me.

"It's not what you think." She took a tentative step toward me, gripping my fingers tight.

Those are not the words I wanted to hear.

That they were the same words I'd said to her weeks ago at Red Hart fueled my growing rage.

"Really." I laced the words with sarcasm.

Natalie ignored my petty show. "His father is sick."

"Bill." I already knew that. But something in her eyes...I sucked in a fast breath. "Terminal?"

"Yes." Natalie considered me. "I believe Eve told you about him."

I raised an eyebrow, aiming to cover my surprise. "I didn't know you two were still in touch."

Natalie gave me a wide grin and bumped my shoulder with hers. "Don't know much, do you, Jon Snow?"

"What?" I didn't bother to hide my confusion.

Natalie rolled her eyes. "Trust me to find a man who doesn't binge watch a second time."

"Sweetheart, I just work. I don't have the energy to do much else." The moment the comment left my mouth, my cheeks heated. I ran my hand over my head, scraping my nails through my scalp. It did little to cover my discomfort

"I seriously doubt that." Natalie said. Her eyes lit with the mischief I knew, and my heart- and cock leaped. "He– Pierce, he gave something to his father. First it was blood transfusions a year ago. A few months back he donated a lobe of his lung."

Both of my eyebrows aimed for the antler chandelier. "What?"

There was no debating it; I've seen his scars for myself. That the self-righteous, spoiled boy would do something for someone— anyone—else, including the father he frequently professed to hate sat poorly with me. Yes, he might have dealt with his father's impending mortality in a different reaction than held to his character but...this was Pierce.

Not someone from the street who might have been more giving, but a kid who had grown into a honestly dreadful adult, and one I had to pry away from Eve with every passing year. Somehow, they were attached to each other, while Travis and I brokered an impromptu truce that wavered on his best behavior.

"He's not what you think," Natalie murmured. She took a small step to close the distance between us, and hesitated. "Do you want a cup of coffee?"

No. I just want you.

I raised a shoulder and admitted a silent defeat.

CHAPTER 13

A few minutes later I was seated stiffly in an armchair, staring at the fire over a rough hewn and varnished coffee table, likely homemade. Her late husband's ghost swept around the room, and I hoped I could hold up my end of the bargain.

Baskets lined the side of the fireplace, each holding a different sort of wood, pinecone stack of coloured, fluffy blankets. The fire burned low. I grabbed a few longs from a basket and made a neat stack that caught all too easily. My gaze roamed the board, open space as I stood, stretching.

Her history surrounded me. Emotions overflowed my mind that I hadn't dealt with since I'd walked out of my father's house too many years ago. Instead of facing them, I filled the time browsing over her incredible library. When Natalie curled onto a next of pillows beside me, the internal temperature increased tenfold.

Natalie handed me a steaming coffee mug and noted the dictation I'd sent my attention. "What was the last thing you read?"

"Elking Mad, A Guide to Husbandry and Beyond. If I ever get a chance to put what I've learned down, I'll make up a journal called Getting Elked and mail it to you." I spoke into my coffee. "I'm not much of a reader. Sorry."

"Don't be." Natalie smiled. "I'm sure you would read if you had more time."

"Maybe." Would I? I didn't know the answer to that.

Natalie sipped from her mug. "How have the elk managed? Or have you managed?"

"We're doing the best we can." I ran my thumb around the edge of my coffee mug, tracing over the dancing deer that sported bow ties, each holding a balloon. Natalie's gaze weighed on me, tracking the actions. Her attention warmed me, and I took the plunge. "I'd love to have a look at how you set up everything, make sure I'm doing it all right."

Silence filled the small space between us that grew until a log cracked and tumbled back into the fire from the neat pile I had built.

"No invitation, then." Natalie hid behind her mug.

I put my own down on the coffee table and turned to her, wrapping my fingers around her knee.

Moment of truth.

Natalie didn't react in shock at my touch, but she let me squeeze her in a familiar action, as my body began the halting process of reacquainting with her body. The risk was huge, touching her without her permission after how we had parted ways. The tension of our last meeting brought my stomach back to its churning state, but I ignored it. Unless she pushed me away, or said anything at all, I didn't want to stop.

I closed my hand around her mug and extracted it from her grip to place it next to mine on the coffee table. Moving with exquisite slowness, I placed my other hand on her hip, giving her all the chances in the world to object. Shifting my weight, I bent over her, pushing both our boundaries in a desperate bid to read a truth, any truth, in her eyes.

Give me a reason to trust you.

Give me a reason to stay.

"No lies, Natalie. If you want an invitation, then you have to show me I can trust you."

"I'm not sleeping with Pierce. In fact, you're the first person I've been with since my husband died." Her azure gaze swam with emotion, mixed and undecipherable. She didn't fight my stare, or try to look away, and neither did she balk at my touch.

Natalie shivered, her gaze locked on mine, and leaned forward to close her small hands into loose manacles around my wrists.

Not fighting, not pushing away. Just there.

They were the only jewelry I was prepared to wear.

"I'm sorry about your husband. You never deserved to be alone, especially for so long."

Country life could be such a lonely existence, particularly if she was doing it with a full complement of farm hands, but from the look of the main house, she held to a similar set of house rules as Eve.

For the first time I wondered how they got along. It hasn't occurred to me to ask Eve about her. Was Rachel a part of their friendship group? I had no idea and sat back only just starting to understand the breadth of my ignorance of the social requirements of the ranch.

I worked hard so I didn't have to deal with the nitchy bullshit of the cowboys. Rodeo riders were the worst. But that I'd missed such a crucial part of RHR's family life, albeit the extended one, floored me.

"You're ruining me, you know that, right?" I murmured, leaning my forehead to hers.

Natalie arched forward, tilting her head back until her lips grazed mine.

"You can't have everything your way, Jude," she whispered, breaking a barrier I hadn't realized I'd erected between us.

A soft growl began deep in my chest, aching to satisfy the craving that rose at her touch. I inhaled a last breath, brushing my mouth over hers.

She tasted of coffee and caramel. Of mountains, fresh air, and home.

Her body softened against mine. I swept an arm past her and shoved every pillow she'd perched on away. They tumbled to the floor as I pushed her back, using my weight as leverage, our kiss flooding my senses with desire and need.

She never fought me, clinging to me in the slow journey backward, raising her thighs to wrap around my hip in her response. Natalie held tight, her hands curved around my shoulders, her fingernails biting through my shirt, but she never broke the kiss as I tipped her backward, pressing her to the leather pillows, covering her with my body. She followed every direction my body asked of her, opening and arching in unspoken invitation.

I released her hip, running my knuckles along her ribs to graze the swell of her breast, bare beneath the thin cotton. "Do you always walk around the house with no bra?"

She opened her mouth to answer, and I gently squeezed her nipple, rolling it between my forefinger and thumb.

Her words became a soft moan I couldn't decipher, but her pleasure was clearly written on her face, in the arch of her back, her curves strainging against the material as I tortured her in the best was I knew.

One more thing I've learnt about you.

I squeezed a little harder, alternating rolling and pinching until she was a writhing hot mess beneath my hands. I used my spare hand to unbutton my own shirt, peeling it back and shucked it to the ground. Her gaze skated over the hard planes of muscle earned from years of endless work that I threw myself into, though the flesh was marred by a plethora of scars I'd never thought about until now.

"I'm not perfect, Nat." I pressed my hips against her heated center, just for the assholic pleasure of hearing her moan. The sound shocked straight to my cock, and I echoed her with one of my own, unsatisfied, for now.

Her fingers tightened on my wrists, as though anchoring herself when I thought she would reach out. She shook her head. "You're perfect to me."

I slipped my fingers along her denim-covered mound, tracing the puffy bump there. Her breath hitched, her hips raised to meet my touch. I flicked open the stud at the top, sliding my hand inside to curl against slick, swollen flesh, her pussy warm, smooth and inviting.

She whimpered, already rocking against my fingers.

I smiled, a dark, almost cruel thing that widened her eyes, or maybe that was my fingers playing in her slicked flesh. My lips grazed hers as I spoke. "I'm going to have so much fun with you." I released her nipple, the bud hard and tight with arousal, and dipped my head to graze it with my teeth and tongue, playing with it as I did her pussy.

She alternated arching against my mouth and fingers, twisting in my hold and smothering small cries behind bitten lips until she lost her rhythm. A shiver began in her core, her fingers tightening around my wrists as she pulled me deeper. But this was a war I waged on my own terms. The heel of my hand lightly brushed against her clit, and my fingers slid deep inside her pussy. I maintained the pressure both inside and out, assaulting her center in an over-stimulating caress that drew moans from her swollen lips. Her nipple popped from between my lips, and I lifted my head to kiss her deep and hard.

Her cry broke, her breath caught and I remembered it. I'd brought up the fantasy of her fucking me in the dark nearly every night she'd been away, the dark hours spent running my fist over my cock, trying to replicate her touch. Nothing worked, leaving me in an exhausted mess and utterly unsatisfied.

Her pleasure rolled over her in a tight wave that left her bucking against my hand, already grinding and seeking more friction. "Greedy girl."

I kissed her hard, and she mewled wordlessly against my lips. She wriggled free of her jeans, kicking her legs free in languid, slow motions as she started coming down from her orgasm. I pushed her thighs apart, sliding down her body to trace over her swollen, flushed tender skin with my tongue, sucking and licking until her hands tangled in my hair.

She yanked at my shoulders, but I refused to let go, pressing her thighs wide, though she was determined to lock them behind my head. Eventually I let her win and slid my hands beneath her ass to lift her closer, burying my face in the warm scent of her.

My cock ached, and I slid my hand into my pocket to extract my wallet and tossed it over my head. I hoped it landed on her chest, and from the scurrying above me, I figured my aim had been good.

A crinkle, and then a rubber pressed against my forehead. I huffed a laugh against her skin. She moaned, rubbing against me, her desperate need gowing. I sucked her clit between my lips, teasing the tight nub of nerves with my tongue, flicking in a furious rhythm as I rolled the rubber over my cock. My fist closed tight around my length, I worked it a few times, pushing myself to the edge then backing off, wanting to be as hard as possible before I was inside her.

Natalie moaned, thrashing her hips against the leather beneath us, pinned by my weight.

The tremors started again, her cry torn and raw.

I slithered up her sweat-coated body, her slick flesh easing my path as I slid fully inside her. Nat's eyes flew open, and she gasped for air as her pussy clenched tight around me. Her body tensed, flexing, and I speared deeper into her, until I rested my thighs against hers, engulfed to the hilt as she rode out the wave of her pleasure and I willed myself not to come.

I wanted to claim her, to know she was mine, but that wasn't a battle I could choose. Natalie would come to me on her terms, and the only battle I could fight was the one that would leave both of us both satisfied and insatiable at once.

Her body fluttered in gentle aftershocks that sent zings of pleasure to the tip of my cock. My balls drew up tight as I began to move within her. My fingers gripped her hips to give me leverage to slam deeper into her. I massaged the sensitive point between hip and thigh, and she moaned, fighting against me for purchase, but this was my battleground, and I'd waited too long to worship her.

I moved faster, my own desire unleashed in the wake of hers. She raised her hips, moving with me, matching my frantic pace until I hit the crest, dangling there in pure pleasure and pain before I plummeted over the edge, my head buried into the crook of her shoulder as I shouted her name.

I breathed in the scent of Natalie's skin and licked salt from the crook of her neck. She shivered in my arms, clinging tighter to me, then giggled.

"Jude, that was—"

"Shh," I murmured, lifting my head to brush a gentle kiss over her soft lips, swollen from our lovemaking. "Don't."

"Don't what?" She arched lazily. Her legs wrapped around my hips, holding me close. "Don't move? I approve of this strategy."

I laughed softly, and her body reacted to the timbre of my voice. "I have to move eventually, sweetheart. You know that, right?"

"Mmm, but not just yet." She snuggled against me. Her head dropped back, the lines of her face softened.

"God, but you're beautiful. You know that?"

"Blanket."

"What?"

"There." She gestured at the floor and poked my ribs.

Rolling slightly to the side, I flapped at the pile of discarded pillows and finally found the blanket she wanted and threw it one-handed over my back. Pinned between my body and the warm leather of the sofa, I had no idea how she could be cold.

"No, silly. It's supposed to be for you." She rolled her eyes between fits of giggles. "Stay?" Natalie sobered a little, her luminous eyes bottomless.

I fell straight in.

"I'll stay for as long as you want me to." I braced on my forearms, wondering if I'd said the right thing or the wrong thing, or what she wanted to hear.

"I never want you to leave."

If I thought I'd loved her before this, her words left me lightheaded. "Are you sure, Natalie?"

"I'm sure. I missed you too."

"That much, huh?" Able to breathe again, I slipped my arms beneath her and squeezed her tight against my chest. "I need to move, but I'll be back in a second, okay?" I managed to remove the condom and knot it one-handed. Slipping out from beneath the blanket, I left it draped over her. "Don't you dare get dressed." I dipped my head to kiss her hard, long, and walked away with her soft moan ringing in my ears. Butt naked, I turned in a circle and aimed at where I thought the other side of the kitchen might be, ending up in yet another library.

"Other side," Natalie called, her clear voice devolving into a giggle.

I turned around and found myself in the biggest walk-in pantry I had ever seen. Rows and rows of dry ingredients fill the shelves, putting Eve's collection into the meager category. I found the bin. Before I could freeze, I grabbed three blankets from the box and an armful of logs from the basket next to the fireplace.

The fire crackled merrily as I crawled beneath the blankets with Natalie, savoring her bare skin pressed to mine. She hadn't dressed, and I was grateful.

She wasn't. "You're freezing!" She wriggled frantically beneath me, which only sent blood and brain power rocketing to my cock again.

A deep laugh rummbled from my chest as I pinned her, parting her soft thighs with my rougher ones, and sank against her skin, determined to work out which sensual torture she loved best.

"I want you up," I promised, dipping to kiss her and let my fingers go on a little tour of their own, unable to drag my gaze from where hers captured me.

CHAPTER 14

My phone vibrated for the twentieth time in the past day, and for the same number of times, I ignored it. The first message that morning had been the only one I cared about, from Rachel with the information I needed to head back to Red Hart. Calling Gage to say I was out for the night had given me almost as much pleasure as I suspect Gage got from telling Trav the same news. What hadn't given me pleasure was the short conversation that followed.

"I'm heading out with a stock truck tomorrow. Sorry I won't catch you before I go."

Something akin to loss opened in my chest. Every time I found someone, I lost someone else. I swallowed hard. "Pity. I liked having someone around who works as hard as I do. You're welcome back any time, man." It was as close as I could give a handshake considering the distance.

"Appreciate it. And, hey, in a few years you never know where we will be."

I know where I'll be, but I'm not sure I can say the same for you.

I cleared my throat. "Stay safe, don't hurt yourself, and if you get a girl pregnant, be an honest man."

"Wouldn't cross my mind not to."
"That's why we get along."

The conversation ended on that halting note. I'd known Gage wouldn't hang around forever, but I'd hoped for more than a few short weeks over the change of season. Besides, the ex-soldier worked damn hard, and I really did appreciate that.

My single night's reprieve with Natalie passed too fast, and after a quick breakfast and a speedy glimpse at how Granite Falls worked,

I jumped in my truck with a stupid ass grin on my face and a giant coffee top up in my hand.

Natalie pulled out of her drive behind me, and we headed to Red Heart Ranch. Speaking to the man I knew I needed to weigh as heavy on me as it had on the trip up to Canada—to Natalie—and by the time we cleared the trees and customs, I made a call I'd been putting off for too long. Even though it betrayed what I had promised, I had to at least let him know.

Archer picked up on the third ring, his voice rough and crackly as though he'd had a whole lotta caffeine and not a lot of sleep. "Jude." He cleared his throat. "Haven't heard from you in a while."

I set my jaw and tried to push the arsehole factor back. "I could say the same for you."

He coughed on the other end of the line, and reception cut out again. "Fuck. I'm sorry man. It's been hell here. I'm still trying to get back up to you guys. And Eve."

"You could do better." Dammit. I tried to not run my mouth on that one, but it came out anyway.

223

"I probably deserve that, won't I?" Archer's voice was rueful.

"No." I rubbed my jaw with my free hand. Natalie waved in the rearview mirror. "Probably not. I've had problems of my own. You don't need me raining shit down on you."

"I can't really take on anything more than I've already got going, otherwise I'd bear it for you too."

The man was a saint, and we all fucking loved him for it. "I know."

"You don't want my shit." Archer purred. "You do want to know when I'm coming back up home, though."

I shook my head. The Texas Ranger cut to the chase too fast for my liking, but with the workload he had going on, I didn't doubt that he needed to make each call quick and to move onto the next problem.

"I understand why you can't. But you do need to know that she's—"

I paused, still unwilling to break the trust Eve had given me. I ballsed up for the moment. It was why I'd made the call after all. It wasn't

224

like I was a social butterfly, and Archer not only knew that, but he didn't have enough time to deal with veiled bullshit, but he'd have to put up with mine for a little longer.

"She's...not okay."

"I couldn't make it back for the funeral. Either of them."

Pure regret reached me from half a country away, and I swatted it away. Archer really did have his hands full, and I'd love him to drop everything, but the bottom line was that the Ranger would always have his hands full.

"It's a bit more than that." I hesitated.

The internal debate ate at my soul, but I had promised Eve and I refused to break that. If Archer wanted to find out what problems had risen in his wake, then he needed to get his ass up to Montana and help fix them.

"You're not gonna tell me shit, are you?" Archer sighed. His frustration was evident in that single, strained breath.

I smirked in a sadistic grin only I could see. "No."

"It's gonna be awhile before I can get up there, Jude. No matter what I want to do, I have a duty here that I can't leave, not yet. I'm working on that."

"You have a duty of care to your team. But what about the woman you've left alone? Isn't she worth more than your entire unit?"

She'd better be.

There was only one answer to that loaded question.

"Yes. She is," Archer answered quietly. "And...I know. We work hard, but I don't see it stopping any time soon."

"At least call her. Or message her." I had to say something. The inaction was crippling, but I pushed it aside.

"I have been." Surprise laced his words. "Didn't she say? Half the reason I'm so fucking tired because I spend all night talking to her."

That brought a smile across my face. I didn't know why she hadn't told me that she was in contact with Archer, and maybe she had assumed the knowledge. But the fact that he was messaging her set my heart alight with a little bonfire, with him its central theme.

"Are you sexting my Eve?" I couldn't help the broad smile that spread across my face.

"Ask her yourse—"

"Or sending her nudes?" I meant to keep the humor out of my voice as I waited for his response. Tears gathered in the corners of my eyes as my shoulders shook.

Archer paused again, and when he spoke, his voice was carefully neutral. "You know, I've got work to do, Jude."

I'm sure you do.

My brain couldn't risk delving into exactly what that was, but I barely contained the laughter building within my chest.

"All right, then." Archer signed off.

He left me sitting in my truck, howling with laughter. Tears ran from my eyes as I waved back to Natalie and let go of the heartache I've been clutching to for an age. The understanding that I didn't have to stay on my own, or need to keep space between me and the rest of the world crashed into me.

Red Hart had been on tenterhooks for a while, and before that, I'd still be in the subspace existence of daily work.

Eat, sleep, repeat.

But now...now, I had someone to share that time with and fledgling as our relationship might be, the thought of sharing that existence with Natalie brought me out of survival mode for the first time in nearly fifteen years.

I sobered at the next call I had to make.

"Trav," I spoke before he did "Rachel is coming round. Got some news on what's happened to our herds."

"Yeah, I know," Travis muttered down the line. "She's already here." He didn't sound any happier than I had expected.

"Good. I'm bringing Natalie back. You can apologize when she gets there."

Travis was silent for a handful of strained moments. "I'm sorry, man. I— see you soon."

He hung up before I had a chance to answer, and the last of my mirth fell away.

Travis might have a bit of apologizing to do when we arrived at Red Hart, but taking his ego down a notch wouldn't hurt. I knew Rachel would be there for him.

As much as we had lost so many family and friends, what the twins had suffered in recent abuse, and grief, it was all coming back, and we were a family at Red Hart once again.

CHAPTER 15

I pulled into Red Heart, followed closely by Natalie. Apparently she didn't care if her truck was covered in dust, though I would be the one washing it later. A familiar black truck was parked next to travel between Travis and Rachel's vehicles in the yard.

My chest tightened. No matter how much of a saint Pierce appeared to have become, my trust for him didn't even make it to the bottom of the charts. I didn't want him around our girl, and I sure as hell didn't want him on the ranch. He didn't belong on Red Hart land, and he had already caused enough problems between Eve and Archer to be welcome for long.

His back was to me, facing Rachel. Travis leaned against the veranda. I had stayed away for a single night and look how much had changed—or maybe I was only just seeing the changes happening right in front of me.

I straightened my shoulders into a hard line and slammed the door to my truck. My boots ate the distance between the invader and me and my truck. Natalie caught my hand, weaving her slimmer fingers through my roughened ones, slowing my pace to match hers.

"You need to be nice, remember?" She turned up a cheeky grin.

"Only for you, sweetheart."

Natalie bounced a little in her steps beside me. "I wouldn't have it any other way."

"You really are a little brat, aren't you?"

"Always." I didn't need to look down to see the mischief that lit her eyes.

"We'll have to do something about that later on."

Natalie squeezed my hand and said nothing.

Travis raised one hand in our direction. His half-hearted wave let me know just how guilty he felt, and the beating his ego had taken.

Good.

I gave Natalie a push over to Trav. "I think he has something to say to you."

She gave me a hesitant glance over her shoulder as she moved forward, her steps shorter and with less bounce.

Trav's gaze zeroed in on her, and she halted, reaching back. I caught her fingers, drawing her to my side. My glare focused on Trav, leveling him with a hard stare that bordered on outright animosity.

Get your head out of your ass, I mouthed to him over her head.

Trav grinned and rolled his eyes.

Movement in my periphery shifted my attention back to Pierce. Rachel stood with her arms folded across her chest, though Eve's expression was much more welcoming. She answered something I couldn't hear and pushed gently past him, her smile blossoming as she raised her arms in welcome.

Pierce twisted to follow her gaze, his face awash in unmistakable anger, before it cleared into the serene, blank face he presented to the world. I held my own response back, recognising the mask and trusting my gut that he wasn't worthy of the sainthood both Eve and Natalie had bestowed upon him.

Asshole.

Natalie blinked. "What?"

"Did I say that out loud?" I murmured for Natalie's ears only.

Her cheeks turned the cutest pink. I filed that response away for later.

Eve cleared her throat. "Rachel said that she told you what had happened?"

I nodded, my eyes flicking up to meet Pierce's. "Yeah. She said someone poisoned the deer." He returned my stare with an unsettling.

"Yes, but it's not what you think. Someone," she stressed the word, "pushed darts or tainted tips into the deer. Hence the open wounds we saw. There were two people here that day, that same day Trav said the deer were looking a bit mangy. Do you remember that?"

I nodded; it was the morning after I'd come back with Natalie, and it was burned into my memory. "Of course."

"But Pierce is only responsible for one of those occurrences."

I raised my eyebrows. "Enlightened me."

Natalie bumped my ribs with her shoulder, and I returned the gesture a little too hard. Maybe that chance to punch Pierce had finally arrived.

"The deer was drugged by Bill, and his son knew nothing about it." Eve paused, her eyes sweeping my face but I denied her the reaction she sought. "The other part was copper, Jude. It looks like some of the piping that Pierce helped me replace a while back, to exuded the copper that has contaminated the water source in their troughs here at the barn. I need you to help me dig it all out and replace it. It's been over supplementing the deer and has caused a lack of growth, and some other smaller, but not irreparable damage. Rachel tested everything, and it took us a little while to sort it all out. I'm sorry to have kept you in the dark, but I was pretty sure you would run off to Blackhill and do something...well. Something not so good to an old man who has lost his control over his life."

Grief filled her eyes, and I was sickened that she wasted it on fools like MacQaid and his equally worthless son.

A part of her explanation niggled at me. "I don't remember Pierce helping you with anything."

Eve turned pink. "It was a few years ago, back when—" She shot a look at Natalie then another over her shoulder to Travis. Natalie caught her eye and wandered discreetly out of hearing distance. "Back when you had a dalliance with a certain rodeo bunny."

It was my turn to turn pink. I coughed into my fist. "Yeah. I do remember that. But I was only away for a week, Eve, the second time in years that I'd left the farm. Why does everything turn to sh—fall apart while I'm not here?" I raked a hand through my hair, dragging my nails through my scalp. The sensation prickled my nerves, waking me up. "Sorry. I just—"

"I know." Eve raised a shoulder and tilted her head to one side. "So stop leaving us, huh?" Her playful grin strained at the corners. Grief still held a shadow over her, but not as much as it had before.

I reached out and pulled Eve into a giant bear hug.

Her hands pressed against my back, tapping a little. "Can't breathe."

I laughed, lightening my hold on her, and cupped her cheeks, checking her face over. "Are you going to me okay?"

She nodded. "Yes."

There was truth there, amongst the shadows, though I was glad she hadn't lied to me.

"Good." I said roughly "Because I had a talk with Archer on the way home."

I watched the last shadows fade away at his name, replaced by a look of pure horror, a battle I suspected she fought on two fronts. "Did you?" she whispered faintly.

"I did. Don't worry. I did as you asked and kept your secret. That's your story to tell, Eve. Between him and you. I just pick up the pieces." I gave her a gentle smile, and she sighed her relief. "He did say something about sending messages in the middle of the night."

"Oh." Her voice dropped to little more than a whisper, though her cheeks blazed. "I thought he would keep it between us."

I huffed a laugh. "To be fair, I asked. Actually, I pushed and was a bit of an asshole. But I wanted to make sure he was looking after my Eve."

She put her hands on her hips pulling out of my right. "Your Eve?"

"You've always been my Eve." I gave her a dopey grin and probably looked like a kid in love with a school teacher.

Natalie rolled her eyes at me behind Eve's back and Travis' expresion wasn't much better. I suspected I'd be wearing that one for a while between the pair of them, but I didn't care.

"And he's always going to be my honey." Natalie slid under my arm and snuggled at my side. "Your brother apologized."

"Finally," Eve and I spoke together.

Natalie pressed a kiss to my shoulder and looked up at me. "Thank you," she murmured.

"My pleasure," I said on automatic. "What for?"

"For making me part of your family." A small smile curved her lips.

I couldn't deny the need to press my mouth against hers and taste her again. Having her by my side at Red Hart felt just as good as it did in her own home. For the first time, I realized how comfortable I'd been off Red Hart land during my time at Granite Falls. I stared at the mountain that towered over the ranch house, working through in my mind where her home sat on the other side, though the land looked different. It really wasn't that far. Maybe that was why I didn't get jittery there.

Or maybe it was because of her.

By the time I raised my head, everyone had moved away, heading into the big house. Well, nearly everyone.

Pierce stood alone, his hands dangling by his too-lanky sides, over dressed and out of place. The same sneer he'd worn before crossed his face before it returned to his mask. I'd honestly forgotten he was there, but maybe with his family falling apart around him, seeing ours growing closer together had been the final straw.

I met his hard as flint gaze head on. "Sabotage isn't neighborly, Black Hill." Detaching from Natalie, I took a step in his direction. "I don't care what you've done for your father. You're both poison, and neither of you are welcome here again."

"Yeah? You're going to need my help soon enough. Don't think you can come and ask for it, or for anything else."

"What I want," I swallowed down bile and the need to punch him, "is for you to get the fuck of Red Hart land."

Pierce's sour expression turned feral, and this time, it stayed there.

I will see what's under that mask one day.

I just hoped it wouldn't be anytime soon, or wreak havoc on Red Hart before I could dissuade him from coming back. Pierce epitomized the sort of bad smell that no threat kept away for loong.

His dead-eyed gaze sent an fear-laced arrow to my heart as he strode to his too clean truck and left in a cloud of dust.

Eve huffed and mumbled something to Trav. Her twin kissed the top of her head and shooed her inside.

I turned back to find the girls clustered behind me. Before I'd thought it through I wrapped my arms around them all, squeezing until one by one they wriggled free. Natalie started at my side, and I kissed her again, needing to feel something permanent when everything about Pierce seemed determined to rip it all away.

Rachel towed Eve inside, chatting animatedly with her, leaving Trav between us and the door. His gaze swung between Natalie and me, his face an indecipherable swirl of emotion.

We stood beneath that assessing gaze, unflinching, and I had never been prouder of the girl who could face down my best friend.

Finally, he cleared his throat. "This is the regular thing now, is it?"

"It is." I tightened my arm around Natalie. "Thanks for the apology."

Trav's gaze shifted from me to land on Natalie. "She deserved it. I was an ass."

"Yes, you were." Nat gave him an impish grin and leaned forward to kiss his cheek.

Trav looked at her in something akin to shock. "Keep him in line, huh?"

"I can do that." She tilted her head back, attitude sparkling in her ocean deep gaze.

"What have you done?" I groaned as Trav made his way into the house.

"You know, I think that's the longest speech I've ever heard you make," she said, still searching my face with that speculative gaze.

"Probably."

It was a one off, and I was unlikely to repeat a diatribe like that any time soon. Following her into the ranch house, I recognised things that had changed, seeing the
242

people who made up Red Hart with new eyes.
Eve and Rachel gave Travis hell as he made his
way on a single crutch to the kitchen, teasing
him mercilessly. He gave back as good as he
got, laughing when he made Rachel blush to
the roots of her hair.

I glanced down at the head of dark auburn
hair tucked into my side. Maybe if someone as
stubborn and set in his ways as Trav could
change, there was hope for an introvert with
his heels dug into the land he loved, the place
he felt most at home.

Now, I shared that love with a woman I
adored, with a new place to discover. Maybe
that change wasn't so impossible, after all.

Maybe I could, too.

A Note from the Author

If you enjoyed Jude and Natalie's story,

continue reading Red Hart Ranch in

SUNDOWN ON THE RANGE

with Travis and Rachel's story

246

Each Red Hart Ranch book will have its own food, and I'd loved to include the comfort foods you love (especially if you're willing to share your own recipes in print!). Call outs will be my newsletter.

You can sign up here:
https://BookHip.com/CNMQFX

LOVE NOTES

CINNAMON & PUMPKIN SCROLLS WITH BUTTER AND BROWN SUGAR CENTER

These gorgeous and moreish scrolls were originally an autumn treat from our own vegetable garden but the more I thought on it, the more they seemed to be a Red Heart dish. I also ran a comp in my reader group Sofia's Sweet Sirens. And the best part? No yeast required.

3 ½ cups all purpose flour

¼ tsp baking soda

½ cup milk

2 large eggs

Pinch salt

2 cups stewed pumpkin

249

¾ brown sugar

75g butter plus some for glazing

Cinnamon sugar to taste

¼ tsp ground cloves

Preheat oven to 170C

Mix stewed pumpkin, flour, baking soda, eggs, cloves and salt in a large bowl. Drizzle milk in and continue to mix until you achieve a doughy consistency.

Turn out onto a floured board and knead, folding the dough into quarters and rotating. Repeat until the dough is layered. Roll out to 1/2cm thickness and cut into long strips.

Melt butter and brown sugar and brush onto strips. Sprinkle cinnamon sugar over the top to taste. Roll and set into baking dish. Glaze with remaining butter and cinnamon sugar mixture.

Bake for 25 mins or until a poked skewer comes out clean. Rest in dish to cool and drizzle with butter icing or cream cheese icing if desired (actually found these were rich enough without the icing, but if you're a sweet tooth, dive in!).

These are tiny oaty biscuits similar to ANZAC cookies, but small enough to fit in a school or work lunch box.

1 cup all purpose flour

1 cup rolled oats

1 cup brown sugar

½ cup shredded coconut

125g butter (melted)

½ cup golden syrup

1 tablespoon water

¼ baking soda

½ cup sultanas or raisins

1 tablespoon orange zest

Preheat oven at 375F

Line two biscuit trays with greaseproof paper.

Melt butter and stir in baking soda and golden syrup. Combine dry ingredients and add butter mixture.

Roll into walnut sized balls and place evenly spread on baking tray. Press lightly with a fork and bake at 375F for 15 mins or until golden brown. The longer they are left in, the crunchier they will get.

Neighboring on cattle farms, Red Hart often serves roast beef with baked veggies to fill the bellies of the hard working cowboys who fill Eve's table every night. I've added Yorkshire Pudding as it's one of my faves and it fills our family table every few weekends.

ROAST BEEF

Pre-heat oven to 375F

Pat beef down to dry and place in baking dish.

Option: make small slices in the top and slide in whole, peeled garlic cloves to taste.

Rub with olive oil and sprinkle with salt.

Cut 1 full bulb of garlic in half cross ways to give a flower effect and bake at the bottom of the roast beef.

Bake for an hour per 2 lb at 375F

ROAST VEGES

These can be as varied as you like and baked at the same time as the beef. Root vegetables and pumpkin work well. Cut into desired portions and spread around the roast inside the baking dish up to 90 mins before the roast is ready. The denser the vegetables, the longer they take to cook, such as potatoes.

Cut roast slices on a board and serve next to roast veges, gravy and yorkshire puddings.

2 cups self raising flour

Lard from previous roast or current roast

2 eggs

⅓ cup milk

Spray patty cake tray well with oil.

Using heat from roast beef and veggies.

Mix all ingredients in a bowl until combined. PLace a ½ tspn cold lard (or hotr if none stored) into the bottom of each patty cake divot. Half fill each patty cake with flour mixture.

Bake for 20 mins or golden.

It is best to put these on toward the end of the roast cook, and serve in a bowl hot next to gravy. Can cover with a cloth to retain heat until the rest of the cook is finished.

ACKNOWLEDGEMENTS

Jude's story has been a while coming and I've loved every minute of getting inside his head. Though as with every character I secretly adore, drawing him out took more time than I expected. In the middle of this book I decided to learn to dictate and while I'm by no means proficient, it certainly helped get the raw words down faster. Even so, the Red Hart introvert dug his heels in tight and refused to come out. Anyway, I coaxed him with a certain redhead, a tribe of resistant elk and a whole lotta coffee.

But those weren't the only things that helped Jude's story see the light of day. My Crit Chicks girls saw him in several states of dishabille, poked and pointed until he shone

257

and I am eternally grateful. Without your eyes,
Jude would be a checked-shirt wearing cowboy
bum and would never have made it off the
ranch to meet Natalie.

My SOS girls. You girls are my sisters in every
way though we circle the globe a few times.
Thank you for your ears, virtual coffees and
5am calls. Here's to Hawaii 2024!

Heather, my most amazing editor. Jude and I
would be in a hell of a mess without your eye.
Thank you for the time you spent on this
project, and I know how exhausting this period
is for you. Sending love and hugs and promise
to edit my dictated notes a whole lot better
next time!

Hubs and kid tribe, where would I be without
you? Thank you for making me spend time
away from the screen and for making me watch
The Mitchells until I cried (both happy and
emotional tears. If you haven't seen this, you
must. Also, mind my weird sense of humor).
Furbies forever.

Sofia xx

About the Author

USA Today Bestselling author Sofia Aves writes fast-paced police romances, sizzling military units, steamy cowboys with a Montana backdrop and the occasional cheeky god. She loves reading Indie authors and hides her collection of college romance books beneath an ever-growing TBR pile. Sofia is the marketing manager for Romance Writers of Australia and has a regular author marketing column in their monthly magazine. She writes kidlit for charity and has over eighty publications across three not-so-super-secret pen names.

Sofia is a mum of three crazies in a returned veteran household, and has an overly large fur baby who thinks she's a teacup puppy.

After eighteen years of planning and dreaming, Sofia and her husband will put the finishing touches on their very own alpaca park this year. Sofia lives near Brisbane, Australia.

Sign up to <u>Sofia's newsletter</u> and get a free Blue Blooded Brothers book.

Haven't read the Z Boy's prequel? Get it for free here:

<u>A TABLE FOR TEN</u>

<u>www.sofiaves.com</u>

Follow Sofia on

<u>BookBub</u>

<u>Twitter</u>

<u>Instagram</u>

SERIES

BLUE BLOODED BROTHERS

RED HART RANCH

TEXAN DEVILS

CHRISTMAS ROMANCE

SHORTBREAD SHAKEDOWN

SECRET SANTA

PARANORMAL ROMANCE

TRICKSTER'S LAW

A PORTRAIT IN ASH & LACE

BLUE BLOODED BROTHERS

COLLISION

book 1

POLITICS & PAPERWORK

Novella

BLINDSIDED

book 2

SENTINEL

book 3

IMPACT

book 4

RECKONING

book 5